Lock Down Publications and Ca$h
Presents

I0666782

The Daughter
of a
Cartel Boss
The Rotten Apple

Written By
SAYNOMORE

SAYNOMORE

Lock Down Publications
P.O. Box 944
Stockbridge, GA 30281
www.lockdownpublications.com

Like our page on Facebook: Lock Down Publications
www.facebook.com/lockdownpublications.ldp

Stay Connected with Us!

Text **LOCKDOWN** to 22828 to stay up-to-date with new releases, sneak peaks, contests and more…

Like our page on Facebook:
Lock Down Publications

Join Lock Down Publications/The New Era Reading Group

Visit our website:
www.lockdownpublications.com

Follow us on Instagram:
Lock Down Publications

Email Us: We want to hear from you!

PROLOGUE

Estabon sat in his chair, smoking a Cuban cigar in the back of his house as he talked over the phone to his brother, Juanito Sanchez.

"Emilio's plane should be landing within the next two hours. He is coming so y'all can discuss the future of our cartel in America."

"I will be waiting on his arrival, but as I told you before, I have everything under control in America." Estabon puffed on his cigar before talking.

"There are reports that you are under investigation for human and sex trafficking, along with kidnapping. The Ochoa Cartel has been a ghost in Mexico to El Paso, Texas, throughout California. Now in New York City for the first time, our cartel is under investigation, so again Emilio is coming to New York to see if we have a future in New York City." Juanito shook his head and took a shot of brandy he had on the table as he looked around his restaurant at everyone.

"Estabon, I look forward to seeing Emilio."

"Good. I'm sure he is looking forward to seeing you too. Juanito, make sure you call me when he arrives."

"I will make sure I call you, brother."

"Good." Estabon hung up the phone and stood up. Estabon was sixty years old, five-nine and slim, with gray and black hair. His full goatee was also gray and black, he had dark brown eyes and his skin tone was brown. He walked with a wooden cane, and he was the boss of the Ochoa Cartel in Medellin, Colombia, running the biggest cocaine operation in the world. Estabon lived in a thirty-million-dollar home, with his own personal army watching his property twenty-four hours a day. He is wanted by multiple countries internationally for trafficking—sex, guns and drugs, kidnapping, murdering and much more.

The Stratos 718X private jet landed in New York City at 9:00 pm. When Emilio and all three of his men stepped off the private jet, there was a 2024 Rolls-Royce Ghost waiting on them. Emilio took a deep breath and said, "America… I hate this fucking country. Come, let's see what my dear old uncle Juanito has going on."

It took forty-five minutes for Emilio's car to reach the luxury five-star restaurant that Juanito owned. When Emilio stepped out of the Rolls-Royce Ghost Juanito walked up to him and gave him a hug and kiss on the cheek with a smile on his face as he looked into his eyes.

"Emilio, tell me, how was your flight?"

"It was beautiful. I had a chance to see the countryside."

"America is beautiful, you are going to love it here. Come inside, I have food and a bottle of Château Margaux 1996. This wine is to die for."

"I'm sure it is." Emilio looked at all the people inside the restaurant. Everyone was there for him. He waved at a few people and sat at the head of the table, along with Juanito. Juanito smiled as he poured Emilio a glass of the Château Margaux 1996 wine. Emilio took a sip and smiled.

"You are right, Uncle. This wine is to die for. So, Uncle, let's talk business."

Juanito lowered his head and lit his Cohiba Royale cigar before talking.

"Let's talk business then. What are the reports your father wants to know?" Juanito puffed on his cigar as Emilio talked.

"There are no reports, just a message." Emilio took a sip of his wine.

"And what is this message, Emilio?"

"New York City has the FBI and maybe the DEA knocking at our front door. You are under investigation. From tonight on, the Ochoa Cartel will no longer operate in New York City." Juanito placed his cigar down in the ashtray and looked into Emilio's eyes.

With an angry voice, he said, "Let me fucking tell you something. I run New York City. I don't give two flying fucks that Estabon runs the deadliest cartel, don't nobody tell me what the fuck to do. He's on the other side of the world, hiding behind his five-thousand-man army, and where the fuck am I? Right here in the open. You go tell Estabon I said fuck his message and you and your men can get the fuck out of my gotdamn restaurant right fucking now." Juanito stood up with a bloodshot red face and was grilling Emilio.

Emilio stood up and turned around, reached in his pocket and turned around real fast, jamming the knife in his uncle's neck. His uncle fell backwards onto the table. Emilio was on top of him, still pushing the knife deeper inside his neck. Blood was pouring out everywhere on the table. Emilio stood up and looked around at everyone watching him. He wiped the bloody knife off on Juanito's shirt and said, "He was right, that wine was to die for. As of right now, everything in New York is shut down." Before he could say another word, the police were kicking the door in raiding the restaurant. Guns out, they ran right up to Emilio and put the guns to his head, roughing him up a little bit as they handcuffed him.

"Tonight is not your night." Emilio just smiled at the FBI agent and blew him a kiss.

"Don't worry, pretty boy. You are going to have a lot of time to do all of that wherever you are going. Now get him the fuck out of here, book him—murder one." FBI Agent Ross looked around, then he walked up to the table and looked down at Juanito's dead body and shook his head. "We couldn't get you, but it looks like someone else did," he said, then walked off.

Chapter 1

Trayvon sat his dark-skinned, six-foot, muscular built frame in the chair in his office. He had deep, dark waves and a full black goatee, with tattoos all over his body. His brown eyes were focused, watching the news with two stress balls in his hand as the news reporter talked about Juanito's murder outside his restaurant, with about twelve FBI agents walking around in the background. All he could think about was, *someone killed the boss of the deadliest cartel*. He got up and walked to his bar and poured a glass of 2009 Chateau Lafite Rothschild, opened the cigar case that Juanito gave him and lit one of his Cohiba Royale cigars. He took two puffs and walked back to his desk, sat down and took a sip of his wine. "A toast to Juanito's memory," he said to himself.

He'd been dealing with Juanito for the last three years, from murder and kidnapping to extortion and kilos of pure cocaine. As he went to take another puff of his cigar, his phone rang with an unidentified number, after the second ring he picked it up. A deep Colombia assent was on the other end of the line.

"Hello?"

"Hello, Trayvon." Trayvon stood up and walked to his office window before talking, having a deep feeling whose voice was on the other end of the phone.

"You know my name, but I don't know yours. Who am I speaking to?"

"Estabon. Do you know who I am?" Estabon puffed on his cigar as he waited for Trayvon to reply.

"Yeah, I do know who you are, Juanito told me about you."

"Juanito... that was this problem, he always talked to much."

"If you are calling me, then you know he was murdered. But I don't have a clue why or by who." Trayvon puffed on his cigar after saying that.

"Money, drugs, and greed became the recipe for his bloodshed. Juanito was secretly under investigation for extortion, murder, and a number of other crimes, but we can talk about that another time. I'm calling because I need your help, Trayvon, and we are on a very short timeline." Trayvon walked to his desk and picked up his glass of wine and took a sip before talking.

"And what can I do for you?"

"My son Emilio was arrested tonight for Juanito's murder. I need him out before his fingerprints come back. He is wanted internationally in two other countries for human trafficking, gun trafficking, drug trafficking, murder, kidnapping, and much more." Trayvon took a deep breath.

"Send me all of your son Emilio's information and I'll see what I can do. I need to know the name he got arrested under. He will be in court within the next forty-eight hours, so we have to move fast."

"You will have everything you need within the hour."

"Once I get it, I'll see what I can do. I will call you within forty-eight hours."

"Trayvon, I'll be waiting on your call." Estabon hung up and puffed on his cigar as he set his Patek Philippe Caliber 89 watch for forty-eight hours. He began to wait for Trayvon's phone call, hoping to see his only son again, no matter the cost.

***

Trayvon looked around at everyone in the warehouse as he made sure he had direct eye contact with each of them before talking.

"Tonight, Emilio Sanchez was arrested. For y'all who don't know who that is, he is the son of Estabon Sanchez, the head of the deadliest cartel in Medellin, Colombia. I called y'all here tonight because I'm asking everyone here to step into a burning hot kitchen to cross a line they never crossed before."

Rakim spoke up. "Gangster, I been down with you from day one, it ain't no question where my loyalty stands tonight." Trayvon nodded at Rakim.

"And that goes for the rest of us. Whatever we need to do, let's go ahead and pop this bottle, gangster. Enough with the chit chat."

"Word, Lance. Love and loyalty to all of y'all. Check this out, tomorrow before noon this is what needs to go down."

Chapter 2

Porscha walked into the courthouse looking like a real boss bitch. She was black and Spanish with an hourglass body. Her eyes were gray. She had long blonde hair with gold stripes at the tip. She reminded you of J-Lo. Porscha walked up to the court clerk's window. It was early so nobody was in the courthouse, just a few people walking around.

"Hello. How may I help you?" Porscha looked around before talking.

"Hey, I need to know the name of the judge and district attorney that's on the Alverez Sliver case?" Porscha took her sunglasses off.

"I'm sorry I can't give that information out. You have to be his attorney or Alverez Sliver himself for me to release that information to you."

Porscha smiled. She then placed five thousand in cash on the counter

"I really need that information." The clerk looked around before picking up the money, punched in Alverez Sliver's name and wrote down on a piece of paper the judge and district attorney's names.

"Thank you, beautiful." Porscha put on her sunglasses and turned around and walked off. Once outside the courthouse, she got into the white-on-white Jeep Grand Wagoneer and handed the piece of paper to Trayvon.

"I knew my baby girl could get it done." Trayvon looked at the names on the paper.

"And you know this, Dad, I will never let you down."

"I know, beautiful. Now let's go get this job done, we are on a timeline."

Trayvon texted the information to two numbers as his driver pulled off.

***

Rakim had on the Murder One face mask. He watched as Judge Smith's wife and two daughters were getting into the car. He looked at Corey and nodded. Corey pulled his gun out and opened the side of the van door as Rakim cut the car off. Corey jumped out the van and pointed the M16 in Judge Smith's wife's face as he opened up the car door.

"Get the fuck out the car, or you and these girls are going to die right fucking now." She opened the back door and stepped out, getting in the van with both her little daughters with tears in their eyes. Before taking off his mask, Corey pulled out his phone and took a picture of Judge Smith's wife and kids with his gun pointed at their heads and sent it to Trayvon.

***

"Trayvon, this is an open and shut case. There was an FBI undercover agent at the restaurant last night when Alverez Sliver killed Juanito Sanchez. There will be no bond. The district attorney is a bulldog with a star witness, that is the undercover FBI agent." Trayvon pulled out his cigar and lit it and took two puffs before talking

"Can you get me the name of this FBI agent?"

"Yeah, the district attorney turned it over to me early today with his case file. Let me get it for you." Attorney Chris Salini pulled up Alverez Sliver's case file and placed it on his desk.

"His name is Paul Ross." Trayvon looked at his phone as it was going off and smiled as he puffed on his cigar looking at the picture.

"Mr. Salini, tomorrow just be in court for Alverez. Salini, I have a strong feeling everything is going to work out for the best." Trayvon was very well respected in New York City and his recipe for respect was murder.

Once in the car, it took him thirty-five minutes to reach the warehouse. When he arrived, he walked into the warehouse and up to Rakim.

"How did it go?" he asked as he gave him a pound.

"Like butter, we have both packages in the back." That's when Lance came walking from the back up to them as he was taking his gloves off.

"How we looking back there, Lance?"

"All five of them are tied down and waiting on the main party to arrive."

"Yeah, but there is one more person that needs to be at this party tonight."

"You got a name and address?"

"Just a name, Lance. Paul Ross."

"Shit, I'm going to go grab that baby now."

"He's an FBI agent so he will be holding."

"Shit, they ain't stopped making gunz when they made his, some are just bigger than others gangster. I'll be back with that baby later," Rakim said as he walked off, holding his gun in the air.

"Lance, I need you and Corey to go bring Judge Smith here to me. District Attorney Croughton is already being taken care of. Porscha is seeing to that personally."

"You know what, Gangster, your daughter is more deadlier than you sometimes. I think she don't have a heart."

"Trust me… she is, Lance, and her heart is ice cold."

"Trust me, I believe you."

Chapter 3

Porscha looked at District Attorney Croughton as he walked out of the courthouse with his black power suit on, talking over the phone. As he walked closer to her, she asked him, "Sir, are you the one who ordered the Uber?"

"Yes, I am." District Attorney Croughton was so lost in his conversation, he didn't notice that was not the Uber he ordered. Porscha got into the car and drove off. District Attorney Croughton hung up the phone and said as he looked out the window, "I believe you are going the wrong way."

"Yes, I know. There was a detour, so I am making a right at the light, sir." When she pulled up to the corner, she stopped. That's when two guys jumped into the car and put their guns to District Attorney Croughton's head.

"Give me your phone and shut the fuck up for the rest of the ride." District Attorney Croughton did as he was told. He closed his eyes and didn't say anything else as he had the gun held to his head.

***

Trayvon looked at his watch, it was 8:30 pm. District Attorney Croughton was tied down to a steel chair with a bag over his head. Trayvon watched as Lance and Corey walked Judge Smith inside the warehouse, right up to Trayvon, his hands were tied behind his back, and he had a gun to the back of his head.

"Tie his fat ass up and let's get this over with." They tied Judge Smith to the chair and pulled the bag off District Attorney Croughton's head. District Attorney Croughton looked at Judge Smith, lost for words. Trayvon let them look around. Before talking, he lit his cigar.

"I'm going to try and make this fast. We are all here for the same fucking reason and if y'all play ball, you can leave here tonight, and you will never see me again." Judge Smith looked at Trayvon.

"I'm not afraid of no street thug or gangster, I don't make deals with your kind." Trayvon smiled as he puffed on his cigar.

"So, what you want on your headstone, motherfucker? The judge that didn't make the deal that cost him his life?"

District Attorney Croughton spoke up "Wait-wait-wait…what deal are you trying to make?"

"A man that knows when to play ball. Alvarez Sliver… I need for him to be released when he go to court tomorrow."

"Wait, I just read over that case this morning, he killed Cartel Boss Juanito with an undercover FBI agent right there. They got him dead to the wrong. There's no bond, there's no getting out of there, not with the witness we have."

"No witness, no case, is what you are saying, District Attorney?"

"It's more to it than just that. We just can't pull a rabbit out of a hat, not with the FBI as a witness." Trayvon nodded his head and pulled out his phone and made a call

"Bring him to me now." He then looked at Judge Smith and smiled.

"Do you feel the same way?"

"I told you. I don't make deals with your kind."

"You know I'ma love breaking you in, Judge Smith." Judge Smith and District Attorney Croughton looked at Rakim bringing a beat-up FBI Agent Ross in the room in just his boxers with his hands tied behind his back. Rakim threw him on the floor in front of them.

"You know, you never heard of a gorilla or a lion being prey to no animal. Why? Because they are apex predators… because they kill what's in their path. The FBI and DEA are like apex predators, but then you got that one motherfucker like me, who don't give a fuck and hunts apex predators like a wolf after a rabbit. District Attorney Croughton, I sent my apex predators at you leaving the courthouse. Judge Smith, we got you leaving the bar, and FBI Agent Ross, we were waiting in your house when you got home. Now, let me say this again. Alverez Sliver needs to be set free tomorrow."

"You have every one of us that's on that case, right here, right now. The ball was never in your court, it's in ours. And like I told you before, I don't make deals with people like you," Judge Smith yelled out.

"Well, you are wrong about two things. One, the ball is always in my court, and two, I don't need no witness to show up for court on behalf of the state." Trayvon looked at Rakim and nodded his head. Rakim walked off and came back and poured gas all over FBI Agent Ross.

"Fuck you, fuck you! I'ma see you in hell, motherfucker," FBI Agent Ross yelled out.

District Attorney Croughton turned his head and closed his eyes, he didn't want to see this.

"This is a must, but we will make our deal. That, I promise you." Trayvon nodded and watched Rakim drop a match on FBI Agent Ross, who was screaming and yelling as he rolled around on the ground, being burned alive in front of Judge Smith and District Attorney Croughton. Trayvon pulled his gun out and shot him in the head in front of them. They watched as his body laid still with flames coming off it as blood poured out of his head.

"Now, let's talk about this court case tomorrow."

"You just killed a good cop in front of us and you want us to make a deal. You animal, you have no respect for human life. I will never make a deal with you. Kill me now, you son of a bitch."

15

"No, Judge. I need you for tomorrow… but let me give you some more motivation to show you I'm not the one to fuck with. The ball is always in my fucking court." Trayvon snapped his fingers. That's when the lights in the back of the warehouse came on. Judge Smith and District Attorney Croughton saw their families tied down to five chairs and Porscha pouring gas on all of them. Judge Smith and Croughton were yelling at the top of their voices, pleading with Trayvon as they saw their families crying.

"Wait, wait, we will make the deal." Trayvon smiled as he puffed on his cigar, looking at them.

"See was that fucking hard? Judge Smith, now that we have that understood, this is how this works. Tomorrow when Alverez is released, I'll let your families go. If he's not released tomorrow morning, you both get the pleasure of watching your families burn alive on YouTube. I'm not doing no more talking, both of you know what is at stake. Test my gangster if you want." Trayvon walked up to Rakim and said something in his ear before walking away. Rakim looked at both the judge and district attorney and walked up to them and put a bag over their heads without saying a word.

Chapter 4

The black-on-black Range Rover was waiting in the front of the courthouse when Emilio walked out the courthouse with all three of his men. He had a smile on his face as he got into the Range Rover. It took them thirty-five minutes to reach the airport. When they got there, Trayvon and Porscha were standing there. Trayvon was smoking a cigar when Emilio walked up to him smiling.

"Trayvon, thank you for whatever you did. I just knew it was over for me," Emilio said as he shook Trayvon's hand.

"It's never over when the home team got the ball in their court. This is my daughter, Porscha, it's because of her I was able to do what I did to get you and your men out."

"Thank you, Porscha. Now come, there's much we must talk about."

"And where are we going to talk at, Emilio? On the plane?" Trayvon looked at Emilio then Porscha.

"Wait, what you mean on the plane?"

"Like I said, on the plane. Come, my father wants to see you face-to-face, there's no need to call him. I talked to him on the ride over here already." Emilio placed his hand on Trayvon's back as they boarded the Stratos 716X private jet.

***

Trayvon stepped off the private jet in Medellin, Colombia. He looked around, then he looked at his daughter and shook his head and smiled as he looked at both black G-wagons waiting on all of them. He took a deep breath.

"Porscha, baby girl. Welcome to Medellin, Colombia. We are at the homes of the deadliest cartels now." Porscha looked around, not saying anything. Emilio stepped off the plane as he put his sunglasses on, looking at his country.

"Trayvon, Porscha, you are going to love it here. Come on, let's not keep my father waiting." It took them forty-five minutes to reach the docks where there was a three-hundred-fifty-one-foot, hybrid powered yacht waiting on them. Once they stepped out the G-wagons, Trayvon saw Estabon Sanchez standing on the yacht's deck in all white, smoking a cigar and looking down at them. As they made their way on the yacht, Estabon walked up to his son and kissed him on the forehead.

"I'm glad you made it home safe."

"It's all because of this man right here, Pops." Estabon walked up to Trayvon and shook his hand

"So, this is the man who kidnapped the judge and district attorney's families just to free my son?"

"Yes, and the judge and district attorney as well, to get my point all the way across to them."

"A man who fears nothing, who don't have the fragrance of weakness on him… I respect that, and who is this beautiful queen I see?"

"This is my daughter, Porscha, it's because of her I was able to get the information on the judge and district attorney to free your son." Estabon walked up to her and took her hand and kissed it.

"Thank you, beautiful, for helping free my son."

"You are welcome, Mr. Sanchez."

"Please call me Estabon. So, Trayvon, what about this FBI guy who put a gun to my son's head? And his hands on him?"

"He is dead, I killed him personally last night."

"You know, Trayvon, I owe you a debt that can never be filled. Please come talk to me in private, we can share a cigar together. My son will keep your daughter company." Trayvon walked up to his daughter and kissed her forehead.

"I'll be back, beautiful."

"Ok, Daddy." Trayvon walked off with Estabon.

Once out of sight, Estabon said, "Let me show you something." Trayvon nodded as he walked to the back of the yacht with Estabon. At the back of the yacht, there were two guys on their knees tied up with their hands behind their backs, with two more men holding P-90s to their heads.

"These two men are the ones who bring the FBI to my doorstep, so here we are now."

"How did you find out?"

"I have a lot of friends, Trayvon, a lot in Colombia." Estabon nodded at his two guys. Trayvon watch as their tied-down bodies fall into the water.

"Did they know you was coming for them?"

"Yes, they did, that's why I drowned them with weights on chains."

"So, why not run? If they knew you was coming?"

"Because a lot of people would have died. Mother, father, sons, daughters, aunts, uncles, friends, a lot of people I would have killed. But let's talk business. I need someone I can trust, someone I can do good business with, in America."

"When you say good business, Estabon, what do you mean by that?"

"I am the cartel, Trayvon. My business is murder, extortion, and kidnapping. I have always lived a nefarious lifestyle, but our business will be drugs, kilos of cocaine" Trayvon puffed on his Cuban cigar before talking.

"How much are we talking about moving?"

"How much can you move?"

"It don't matter, I can move whatever you give me."

"Good, very good, how do twenty-three thousand a kilo sound to you?"

"That's a fair number, that sounds good to me."

"Good. Now, there's one more thing I want to talk to you about."

"And what's that?"

"My family, my cartel… I would like for you and your daughter to be a part of my cartel for what you did for me and my son. You will be the boss in America overseeing it all." Trayvon nodded and smiled as he puffed on his cigar, taking in the blessing he was given.

"Good, now let's go eat, there's much to talk about."

Chapter 5

Trayvon had sixty kilos on the table stacked on top of each other. He looked around at everyone at the table. There were two bottles of wine and two bottles of champagne on ice. He lowered his head as he lit his cigar before talking.

"New York City just became our city. We have an endless supply of cocaine, a hundred percent pure. We have a better grade of cocaine at a much cheaper price. Now you know we are going to have our hard asses, so we are going to have to lay the murder game down real thick to let these motherfuckers know there's a new boss in town. If they don't want to ride our wave, then motherfuckers are going to drown by it."

"What Borough are we stepping on first?" Rakim asked.

"Manhattan… they going to feel my presence first and it's going to be like no other. There's only one person who's going to want to learn the hard way, that fat fuck Roberto Reddinger who think he have Wall Street by the balls, so we are going to send him a message first."

"And what type of message we sending, Gangster?"

"That depends on him. Porscha, you are going to go talk with him and how your conversation go, that's how our message is going to go."

"When you want me to go talk with him?"

"As soon as possible. For the rest of y'all, get the word out because as of right now, it's war on all crime bosses. And as of right now, Porscha is my number two and Rakim is my number three. Remember, we don't ride the wave. We are the wave. Now everyone take a drink to us." Everyone picked up their glasses and took a sip.

***

The white-on-white Rolls Royce Ghost pulled up to the private restaurant. Porscha's driver stepped out and opened the back door for her to get out. She stepped out the Rolls Royce looking like a real boss. She was wearing a Balenciaga hoodie and sweatpants cream with a DeBeers diamond necklace on top of her Connor McKnight t-shirt. She had on six-inch, open toe Red Bottom shoes. She walked inside the private restaurant, holding a white and cream Versace bag in her hand. Two of Roberto Reddinger's guards walked up to her.

"I'm here to see Mr. Reddinger. Let him know Porscha is here." One of his guards walked off as the other one stayed with Porscha, taking in her beauty.

"Sir, you have a Porscha here to see you." Mr. Reddinger looked to the front of the restaurant at Porscha standing there.

"Bring her back here to me, let's see what our guest wants to talk about."

"Yes, sir. I'll go bring her to you right now." Porcsha looked at the six foot two, heavy-set guard walking back her way.

"Come with me, he would like to see you."

"Lead the way." Porscha walked with the guard to the back of the restaurant where Roberto Reddinger was seated. Roberto stood up and shook Porcsha's hand. He really didn't care for black or Spanish people and knowing she was mixed, he disliked her even more. Out of respect for her, he was willing to hear what she had to say

"Tell me, Porscha, what can I do for you?"

"I will get into that in a moment, but first, I have some gifts for you from my father." Porscha opened up her Versace bag and pulled out the case of Padrón Family Reserve cigars and handed it to Roberto, along with the bottle of Château Margaux 1996.

"I see your father knows his cigars and wine, tell him I said thank you for the beautiful gifts. So, tell me, what can I do for you?"

"My father has an endless supply of one hundred percent pure cocaine at a very low price, and he is bringing this to your table out of respect of who you are to see, would you like to do business with him."

"Trayvon has one hundred percent pure cocaine at a low price and wishes to do business with me? Why me?"

"Again, out of respect of who you are."

"I'm going to say no. Let your father know Manhattan is my backyard and it will stay that way. Remind him, some people are meant to take care of the pigs and others are meant to take care of the prize-winning horses. Let him know he is not ready to sit at the table with me." Porscha looked at Roberto and laughed.

"Enjoy the rest of your evening, Roberto." Porscha got up and walked out of the restaurant with one thing on her mind. Murder, and Roberto Reddinger was the one with the target on his back.

Chapter 6

"Mr. Salini, here's the thing. I need friends in high places that will put green before their oath. Judges, district attorneys, cops, even the mayor if we can." Mr. Salini walked to the mini bar in his office and poured himself and Trayvon a shot of Ciróc. He then walked back to Trayvon and passed him the glass before sitting down.

"I know a few people who would take the green over the badge and that will look the other way for the almighty dollar. But for you to… let me see how I can put this, for you to sit at the table, you have to leave the people at your old table alone because their face will be on the line." Trayvon took his shot of Ciróc.

"I can play my part and do that. I just need you to get me the friends."

"I'll make some calls and let them know I have a special client who wants to make a healthy donation to the people that protects the city."

"Thanks for the shot, Mr. Salini, I'll be in touch."

"Trayvon, don't forget my donation. I like doing business with you, your checks always clear."

"How can I forget?" Trayvon said as he walked off. Salini was crooked but the best at what he did

***

"Rakim, I'm not going to call my father every time the wind blows in a different direction. That fat fuck was too disrespectful, he acts like he can't be touched."

"So, how you want to deal with him, Porscha?"

"I want his ass dead, and I'm going to do this one personally. It's time to show a mob boss even he can bleed. And the Jamaicans, I want that turf too we are about to kill two birds with one stone. From this point on, it's war on all crime bosses."

"You know that's going to bring a lot of heat on the city."

"Sometimes, you can't stop the rain when it starts to pour." Porscha walked to the window and looked out it and said again, "Rakim, you can't stop the rain when it starts to pour," as she looked at the city of Manhattan.

***

"You know, Roberto, you should have worked a deal out with Trayvon. Just to test the waters. Never pass up an opportunity to make more money," Tyler Costner said to him as they walked down Main Street

"I don't like niggers or half-breed niggers, so fuck him and his deal. He needs to know his place and it's not at the table with me." Roberto lowered his head and lit his cigar before walking again.

"I made some calls, and I will tell you this. Someone is pushing A-1 grade, one hundred percent pure cocaine at a very low price, and I'm going to tell you now, they are going to take over the city."

"Let me tell you now, Costner, I will kill every nigger I see if just one of them cross the line on my turf. I fucking promise you that."

Porscha rode backwards on the Toyota 650 dirt bike holding a P90 in her hands while Corey raced the dirt bike down Main Street. Porscha had on an all-pink biker outfit with the matching helmet, her body was completely covered.

Corey was in all-black. Corey jumped the sidewalk headed right at Roberto. Tyler looked back and jumped out the way as they rode past Roberto. Porscha pulled the trigger, letting thirty rounds into Roberto's upper body. She then started shooting at his bodyguards, killing them both. Corey jumped back off the sidewalk and made a right down an alley.

Tyler got up and looked at Roberto Reddinger's dead body lying in a pool of blood, along with both his bodyguards. People had their cell phones out recording everything. Tyler looked around, not believing what had just happened. Mob capo Roberto Reddinger was dead, killed on Main Street.

***

Twenty-plus officers were standing around the East River as CSI was investigating the body of FBI Agent Paul Ross, that a fisherman pulled onto shore.

"Can my day get any fucking worse, a fucking dead FBI agent in my city killed, burned and shot in the fucking head?" Detective Flowers walked up to Captain Lawson and Detective Boatwrite.

"Captain, I just received a phone call, there was multiple one-eighty-sevens on Main Street today, about an hour ago."

"There you have it, my day just got fucking worse. Detective Boatwrite, did they say who the victim is?"

"Yeah, mob capo Robert Reddinger and two of his bodyguards was gunned down by two people on a dirt bike."

"You know this is too much right now. Brief me on everything back at the station."

"Yes, sir."

"And look, guess who just joined the party, the FBI. My day just keep getting better and fucking better by the moment."

***

Rude Boy sat in the front of the restaurant with a few more of his homies, eating curry goat. He had his blacks on lock. He and his team were killers, they called themselves Jamaican Hitters. Lance watched them from his car as they sat down eating, thinking they were the untouchables. Lance loaded up his P90 with the switch and drum he put his Murder One mask on and hoodie as he looked at all of them.

"Terry, you ready to lay these motherfuckers down?"

"Nigga, you know I am."

"Good, let's get this shit over with." Terry put his mask on and started up the van. Lance opened up the side door to the van. He drove up right where Rude Boy was and opened fire on them, hitting Rude Boy who tried to run run but his legs didn't cooperate. Rude Boy fell to the ground. Lance jumped out of the van and pointed the P90 at Rude Boy's face.

"This that long kiss goodbye, motherfucker." Rude Boy looked up at Lance and said as he was holding his stomach. "Fuck you, pussy hole, go suck on your mama."

"Suck on this, nigga." Lance let the whole clip go into Rude Boy's chest. He looked around at his dead homies and jumped back in the van as Terry pulled off. People were watching the whole thing play out as if they were watching a movie.

Chapter 7

Chris Salini sat at the table at the five-star restaurant Jean-Georges with Judge Adam Miller, District Attorney Sandi Smith, and Mayor Micheal Rapkin as they all talked and shared a bottle of Chateau Mouton Rothschild 2009 Pauillac.

"Ok, so enough with the small talk, Salini, you called us here for a reason so lay it on us."

"I have a client who need friends in high places." Judge Miller leaned back and lit his cigar before talking.

"Who is this client of yours? Because we take pride of the company we keep."

"Trayvon L. Robinson." District Attorney Smith took a sip of her drink before talking.

"So, he's Black."

"Yes, he is, and very well respected."

"And why should we be friends with him?" Mayor Rapkin asked.

"For starters, this is one reason." Chris Salini wrote a number down on a piece of paper and handed it to Mayor Rapkin. He then said, "My client would like to make a very healthy donation to the good people who is helping to keep our great city of New York safe from thugs and gangbangers." Mayor Rapkin passed the paper around to everyone at the table

"That is a very grateful donation." Everyone nodded at the number. Salini smiled as he took a sip of his wine before talking.

"I forgot to say that number is for each of you." Everyone looked at each other and smiled.

"Salini, what is it that your client does again? I don't believe you told us."

"How about I let y'all speak to him yourselves, how's that sound?" They all nodded in a sign of agreement to meet Trayvon. Salini pulled his phone out and texted him. The text said, "Come inside, back table on the right. Your name is on the list already. You are coming to the Salini party."

Trayvon replied back, "On the way now."

Trayvon's driver stepped out of the Rolls-Royce Phantom and walked to his door and opened it for him to step out. Trayvon had on a gray and black power suit, well-fitted. He had a fresh line up. Just his presence demanded attention as he walked inside Jean-Georges. Looking like a boss, he walked up to the front desk.

"Hello, are you eating alone tonight, sir?"

"No, I'm not. I'm joining the Salini party."

"Your name please?"

"Trayvon Robinson."

"Ok, I see your name right here, follow me and I will walk you to your party."

Trayvon followed the young lady to his party. When they saw him, they were all in shock at how well he carried himself. Salini stood up when Trayvon reached the table.

"Trayvon, let me introduce you. From the right you have Judge Adam Miller, then you have District Attorney Sandi Smith and last, Mayor Micheal Rapkin."

"Nice to meet all of you."

"Likewise, Trayvon, Mr. Salini told us you are looking for friends."

"I am, Judge Miller."

"Please, just call me Adam."

"Well, Adam, I am looking for friends. I think we all need friends."

"So, tell me, what can you bring to the table?" Trayvon smiled before talking.

***

Captain Lawson was sitting at his desk as Detectives Boatwrite and Flowers were briefing him on the cases.

"So, tell me, what y'all got so far on these murders?"

"Sir, this is a takeover. Let's go back to the very first murder. Juanito Sanchez was killed at his own restaurant by Alverez Sliver, or who we thought was Alverez Sliver. But his fingerprints came back, and his real name is Emilio Sanchez, son of the cartel boss over the Medellin Cartel in Colombia," Detective Boatwrite said.

"You have to be fucking kidding me! So, are you telling me Estabon Sanchez's son was locked up in one of our cells and we let him go?"

"Yeah, but that's not all Captain. Emilio Sanchez is wanted internationally by multiple countries for human trafficking, gun trades, and murder, the list goes on and on, Captain. Now the FBI agent who was killed, Paul Ross, was the FBI agent working undercover in an investigation that was a year-long in the Juanito Sanchez case. That's how the restaurant was raided so fast, he was there when Emilio murdered Juanito, but it gets deeper than that. The next day, we received a 911 call saying that Judge Smith's wife Vanessa and two daughters were kidnapped. But when the police got to the scene, there were no signs of foul play, so they brushed it off. The next day, Emilio Sanchez was released from prison and get this. Both Judge Smith and District Attorney Croughton resigned from their positions that same day and both families moved."

"So, they kidnapped the judge and district attorney's families, killed the FBI agent who is a witness to it all and got Emilio Sanchez out of jail by holding the D.A. and judge's families at gunpoint. So does this have anything to do with mob capo Roberto Reddinger?" Detective Flower said.

"It could be one or two things. One, Estabon Sanchez is cleaning up house or two, there's a new boss in the city and this is the start of their takeover. Because keep in mind, not just Roberto Reddinger was killed. Rude Boy, head leader over the Jamaican crew, AKA the Jamaican Hitters, was killed. If you ask me, this is the start of someone's takeover and they are not playing. This is just the outside of the storm we are not in the eye of it yet, sir."

"Fuck me. Ok, look… keep doing what y'all are doing, I need to go talk with the chief about all of this. Keep me posted about anything new y'all come across."

They both said, "Yes, sir," as they got up and walked out of his office.

***

Tyler Costner walked into the Murray Hill Tower Apartments to go see Mannino Caporegime. He walked into the ballroom where Mannino was seating at the bar having a drink as he waited on him. Mannino got up and shook Tyler's hand when he saw him come in.

"Tyler, thank you for coming to see me."

"When Mannino Caporegime calls you, you come."

"Please have a seat and help me put all of this together about Roberto's murder." Mannino snapped his fingers, and the bartender brought them two glasses of gin and ice.

"I really don't know what to tell you, Roberto called me a few days ago and asked me about Trayvon Robinson, because he heard he was moving one hundred percent pure cocaine. I told him I'll look into it. He told me that Porscha came to see him on a business deal and in so many words, he spit in her face. He was very disrespectful to her. I checked out the rumors like he asked me to. We met up the next day, as we were walking. That's when the dirt bike came down the sidewalk, killing Roberto."

"I understand that but let me show you what I don't understand. You see, there is a video uploaded on the internet of the shooting. Let me show you what I mean." Mannino played the video. They saw the shooter point the gun at Tyler, then they pointed the gun at Roberto and fired at Roberto, then his men as they rode off. Mannino stopped the video right there. "See, that's what I don't understand, why not shoot you as well?"

"Mannino, I don't know, I swear to you I don't know."

"I understand, trust me, I do. It's a slippery slope for me, a hard pill to swallow, there's to many unanswered questions here, Tyler."

"Mannino, you have to believe me."

"I really want to, I do, but I can't."

Mannino snapped his fingers, and his bodyguard wrapped a metal wire around Tyler's neck and started to choke him, as Mannino's other bodyguard pulled his knife out and stabbed him multiple times in the chest. Blood was pouring out everywhere. Mannino watched as Tyler took his last breath as he lit his cigar and took a few puffs.

"Dump his body somewhere in the open just in case he did have something to do with Roberto's murder. They will know we ain't laying down. And set up a meeting with Porscha, let her know I want to have a word with her."

"Will do, boss. I'll get on that after I dump his body off in Center Park." Mannino nodded and walked away. He was going to let it be known he was not to be fucked with.

***

The black-on-black Cadillac Escalade Platinum Edition pulled up to the Prism at Park Avenue South Apartments in Manhattan. Porscha's driver stepped out of the Escalade and opened the back door for her to step out. She was wearing a two-piece Gianvito outfit and a pair of Red Bottom six-inch heels. Her fingernails and toenails were painted white, her hair was pulled back, and she had a pair of Versace sunglasses covering her face. Porscha was a bad bitch and she knew it.

"I have a meeting with my father, be back to pick me up in one hour, do not be late."

"Yes, ma'am." Porscha walked into the apartment building right to the elevator, where it took her to the penthouse. Once off the elevator, she saw the two guards that Trayvon had at the doors, she walked past them into the penthouse. She walked up to her father and gave him a hug and kiss on the cheek. He kissed her back on the cheek and forehead.

"How you been, beautiful?" Trayvon asked as he walked her to the table.

"Good, just taking care of the cartel, that's all."

"And how is that going?" Porscha smiled when she thought back of all the drive by shootings and crime bosses that were killed on her orders as she started her takeover

"It's going good. I have Terry moving weight in Castle Hill Houses in the Bronx. Lance is moving weight at Patterson Houses in Brooklyn. We are moving a hundred and twenty kilos a week, two million dollars a week, and it's only been three months."

"Yeah, the numbers are looking good. Matter fact, better than good. I received a phone call from Estabon Sanchez yesterday. He has two shipments coming our way, five thousand guns of all types and some females, twenty of them. He wants us to put them to work and break them in." Porscha shook her head when he said that.

"Porscha, you know, what we signed up for this comes along with it."

"Ok, I'll take care of it. I have a girl, her name is Paris, she runs one of my clubs I'll set the girls up in there and I'll have Rakim take care of the gunz."

"Good, make sure you are on the docks when the shipment arrives."

"I'll be there. So, how are things with you?"

"Good, but don't worry about me. As long as I'm doing my song and dance for the rich and powerful you are untouchable, Porscha."

"Trust me, Father. I know you have my back, just like I have yours."

"I see the conversation with Roberto ain't go too well, but killing him in broad daylight, now that was bold. And the leader of the Jamaica Hitters on the same day, just hours apart from each other. Now *that's* making a statement, Porscha," Trayvon said as he picked up his cigar and lit it.

"I wanted StuyTown and that fat fuck wasn't going to give it up, plus he was so disrespectful, so I wanted his people to know that fat fuck bleed just like the rest of us. And as for Rude Boy, we needed Polo Grounds Towers to buy from us. Now everyone knows they can get down or lay down. Like you said, Dad, we are the wave."

"I did say that, so what's your plans now?"

"I have to go talk with Paris and get ready for tomorrow night."

"Good. I'll let Estabon Sanchez know that we will be ready for tomorrow night and count up fourteen million dollars. We need to make a payment to Estabon this weekend."

"I'll have everything ready by Friday."

"That's what I want to hear and Porscha, watch the body count. We don't need the FBI watching us."

"Father, sometimes murder is a must. Shit, you can't stop the rain when it starts to pour." Porscha got up and kissed her father's forehead as she looked into his eyes. "I love you, Father."

"I love you more, baby girl." Trayvon smiled as he watched his daughter leave the penthouse, knowing she was that boss bitch.

***

"Look, make the fucking grams. Grams, not point five. Not point eight. Point one-zero, and a kilo is a thousand and seven grams, it ain't that fucking hard, this shit is ABC and 123. I need six kilos broke down into grams and forty kilos broke down into eighty kilos, Porscha is coming here, and I don't need to hear her fucking mouth, real talk," Corey said as he looked around at all twenty workers. The females only had thongs on and the guys, just boxers.

Polo Grounds Towers was Porscha's main stash house. She had the workers at Polo Grounds making up all the bags up over the city. Terry got twenty kilos and a thousand and seven grams bagged up, so did Lance and Rakim, so did Paris. Porscha had shit airtight. Corey walked off when he saw that Porscha was calling him.

"Hey, what's up?" Corey walked to the window and looked out of it as he talked.

"How we looking over there?" Porscha asked as she rode in the backseat of her Cadillac Escalade through Manhattan.

"We good over here, we should be ready in the next twenty-four hours to start dropping off to the other Boroughs."

"Good, keep me posted. I'll be there tomorrow to see how things are going for myself."

"Cool, I'll see you tomorrow" Porscha didn't say anything else, she just hung up the phone as she headed to Club Mercedes to talk with Paris.

***

Rakim walked into StuyTown and stopped when he saw two Italian men standing in his path, he walked up to them.

"Y'all must be lost or think you are bulletproof."

"We have a message for your boss."

35

"And who the fuck is my boss?"

"Porscha, or you forgot? Let her know Mannino Caporegime wants to talk with her."

"About what?"

"The fuck if I know. He wants to meet somewhere public where there's a lot of people but where they can also have their privacy. So how do Per Se sound, tomorrow at 3:00 pm." He then reached in his pocket and pulled out a card with a number on it and handed it to Rakim.

"He will be waiting on her call before 3:00 pm."

"I'll let her know," Rakim said as he took the card and walked past them. He didn't trust these noodle eating motherfuckers, just like he knew they didn't trust niggas.

***

Porscha's Escalade pulled up to the front of the club. Her driver stepped out and opened the back door for her to step out, she walked into the club. The club was closed, the doors didn't open until 6:00 pm. She looked around before walking up to Paris, who was by the bar.

"Porscha, I didn't know you were coming by."

"Paris, I didn't know I was coming by. Come let's go talk in private." They both walked to a corner table out of the workers' sight.

"Hey, everything is good. I have a few girls coming to work at the club. I need you to break them in."

"How many are we talking about?"

"Twenty, but they will be flipping Johns. Three hundred a fuck, each girl will bring in fifteen hundred a night. If they don't, it will be bad on their end."

"Ok, but where will they stay at?"

"Don't you have a whole upstairs that's not being used?"

"Yeah, but there's no beds up there for them to sleep on."

"Paris, let me say this before I go. Tomorrow night I'm bringing twenty females here that will be working for me.

When I go upstairs, there should be twenty beds, twenty dressers, twenty mirrors and everything that they need. So, if you have to keep this place closed tonight to get the job done, I suggest you keep this place closed tonight. You have a blank check, get them everything they need. I'll see you tomorrow night." Porscha got up and walked off, not saying another word. Paris knew not to question her anymore. Porscha made the last manager over the club sniff an ounce of cocaine, then she cut the bartender's throat from ear to ear, just because they were friends and she didn't trust her, so she made sure they died together.

Chapter 8

"Detective Flowers, Detective Boatwrite, this is FBI Agent Stallone and FBI Agent Sampaio. They are here to ask y'all some questions about the investigation," Captain Lawson said. FBI Agent Stallone and Agent Sampaio shook both Detective Flowers and Detective Boatwrite's hands before everyone sat down at the table.

"Thank you both for taking the time out to see me and my partner."

"No problem. So, what can we do for you?" Detective Boatwrite asked.

"It's been four months since Agent Ross was killed, and his case done went cold, and that's not sitting well with me or my partner."

"To be honest with you, our cases have went cold as well. The restaurant where Juanito Sanchez was killed was burned down, Estabon Sanchez's son, Emilio Sanchez, was under a fake name, Alverez Sliver. The judge and district attorney that was working the case resigned. Rumors say his wife Vanessa and both of his eight-year-old daughters was kidnapped, along with District Attorney Croughton's wife Jennifer and her son. Not only did they resign, but they also moved out the state, Agent Stallone."

"Yeah, we looked into that, Detective Boatwrite. We had Juanito Sanchez under investigation for the last year, hoping he would lead us to Estabon Sanchez, but that was never the case. So, a week before Juanito Sanchez was killed, we were going to pick him up on organized crime. We had enough on him to put him away for life. Now our CI's in Colombia who was able to get Agent Ross into Juanito's organization, both of them were killed right around the time Juanito was killed. They were drowned, tied down to ship weights. Here are the pictures we got from our contact in Colombia." Agent Sampaio passed the pictures to both detectives to look at.

"So, you think Estabon or his son Emilio had them killed?"

"Yeah, we do, Detective Flowers and we think that he has someone else running things in New York now for him."

"You know, recently there's been a bloody path of murders. Mob capo Roberto Reddinger and two of his guys, along with the leader of the Jamaican Hitters, Rude Boy and three of his guys. And just yesterday, Tyler Costner's body was found in Center Park, he was choked and stabbed to death. So, someone is making moves on all the crime bosses, but who is the question?" Detective Flowers said.

"So, we have to follow the money to find the new boss."

"Wait, what you mean follow the money, Agent Sampaio?"

"When we say follow the money, it means follow the boss. And if I'm right, Mannino Caporegime is or was Roberto Reddinger's boss, so if it's a turf war. Mannino Caporegime is going to have a sit down real soon with someone, because he can't afford to go to war with whoever is running the Medellin Cartel in New York. They money is too long, and they are too powerful," Agent Stallone said.

"So, let's go follow Mannino."

"Let's go, Detective Flowers, it's time to nail theses son of a bitches to the cross."

***

Porscha looked at the card in her hand that Rakim gave her as she was sipping on her cup of coffee.

39

"So, Mannino wants to have a meeting with me?"

"Yeah, that's what his guards said that was waiting for me at the apartments."

"Well, let me not be rude, let me call him." Porscha pulled out her phone and called Mannino after a few seconds he picked up the phone.

"Porscha, I been waiting on your call."

"Have you? So, tell me Mannino, what can I do for you?"

"I don't like talking over the phone, I would like to talk to you face-to-face."

"Ok, that's fine with me, I'll see you at 3:00 pm at Per Se."

"I'll see you then." Porscha hung up the phone and looked at Rakim.

"I don't trust these motherfuckers, have two set of guards on standby for this meeting."

"I'll go take care of that now." Porscha watched as Rakim walked off.

***

Trayvon sat at the table with Judge Adam Miller and Mayor Rapkin as they talked and sipped on a bottle of Thienot Grand CRU Vintage champagne.

"Trayvon, where did you learn to play golf like that?"

"My father, Adam, I been playing golf for years," Trayvon said with a smile on his face as he lit one of his Cuban cigars.

"Trayvon, there has been a bump in the road that you may be able to assist us with," Trayvon puffed on his cigar as he listened.

"What can I do for you, Rapkin?"

"Our good old friend Sandi has been talking just a little too much to the wrong people. The wrong ears have been hearing her conversation and that's bad for all of us, if you understand what I mean."

"I think this is something I may be able to assist you with."

"Trayvon, you are one of a kind. Now trust me, you have to try the steak with the country sourdough boule, with the sour cream. It is to die for, trust me."

"You know what, Adams. I think I'll try that."

"You won't be disappointed. I promise you that."

***

FBI Agent Stallone and Detective Flowers sat in the unmarked car outside of Per Se five-star restaurant. They had been following Mannino Caporegime all morning. Mannino and five of his bodyguards were in the restaurant, they had been there for the last five minutes. It was 2:55 pm. That's when they saw the Rolls Royce Phantom pull up with two Cadillac Escalades, one in front of the Rolls Royce and one behind it.

"Agent Stallone, who you think this could be?"

"The boss." That's when Porscha's driver stepped out of the car and opened the door for her to step out. Agent Ross took pictures of everything. Porscha had six men in suits walking in the restaurant with her, they walked right up to Mannino's table. Mannino's bodyguards stood up around him as Porscha's bodyguards did the same. Both Detective Flowers and Agent Stallone went inside the restaurant to see what was taking place. They sat a few tables back so they couldn't be seen.

"Porscha, come have a seat so we can talk."

"Lead the way, Mannino." Both of them sat down at the table.

"So, you asked me to come, so here I am. What can I do for you?"

"My Capo, Roberto, was gunned down in cold blood, after you had a meeting with him not even a week later." Porscha took her sunglasses off.

"I went to talk with Roberto respectfully. He was disrespectful. I brought with me a box of cigars and a bottle of wine in good faith, and you know what he wanted? Blood in the streets, so I gave him blood in the streets."

"You know Roberto was always a hard ass, and he didn't give two fucks about nobody who wasn't his race, but he is dead and that's the problem we have right now, one of mines are dead."

"I don't see no problem. He stepped out of line, and it cost him his life."

"You are a tough cookie, I see. Here's the thing, Manhattan is my borough and if you want to play in my backyard, you have to pay." Mannino wrote a number down on a napkin and passed it to Porscha. "That number is not negotiable. It's a one-time deal." Porscha pulled the ashtray to her, placed the napkin inside of it and set it on fire in front of Mannino.

"I thought about your offer and said… fuck your offer, I'm in Manhattan to stay."

"Just know I'm not Roberto, sweet cakes."

"As long as you know you can't stop the rain when it starts to pour."

"What can I say, a female that stands on her business."

"Have a nice day, Mannino." Porscha stood up and she and her guys walked right past Mannino's men, right to her car. She looked at Rakim.

"Make sure everyone is on point because these noodle eating motherfuckers are going to try something." She looked back at the restaurant at someone looking at her.

"I'll get on that right away, Porscha," Rakim said as she still was looking at them.

"Good, and make sure you are ready for tonight," she said, before getting in the car.

"I'll be ready."

Detective Flowers and Agent Stallone watched as Porscha got into her car and pulled off. A few seconds later, Mannino and his men left the restaurant.

"So, you think she is the boss, Stallone?"

"I don't know, but whoever she is, Mannino knows she is not to be fucked with, so we need to find out who she is."

"Let's get to it then."

"Yeah, because the way she carries herself, she's standing on business."

***

Trayvon looked around the neighborhood before walking around to the back of District Attorney Sandi Smith's house. It was 8:30 pm, as he picked the back door lock to step inside of her house. Sandi was on the phone and didn't know he was in the house. He hid behind the door as he listened to her conversation.

"I can meet you tomorrow at 10:00 pm on Avon Avenue in the back of the warehouse and yes, I will have all of the documents you asked for on Mayor Micheal Rapkin, and all the illegal activities he and Judge Adam Miller have going on." Trayvon shook his head when he heard that. "Ok, I'll see you tomorrow night." Sandi hung up the phone and walked to the bedroom where she put the bag with all the evidence on the bed. There were tape recordings, pictures, documents and much more. That's when Trayvon walked in her bedroom, gun out, looking at her. Sandi couldn't believe what she was seeing, a gun pointed at her

"So, you are a rat, you are trying to bring the whole house down? Why and everyone is eating?" District Attorney Sandi Smith went to get up.

"Don't get up, stay where you are at. Who the fuck are you?"

"I'm Judge Smith's sister, you remember him, don't you? You just kidnapped his wife and kids and killed an FBI agent in front of them. So, let me guess, Miller and Rapkin sent you to me, their little pet dog?"

"I'm no one's pet dog, and I let your family go like I said I would."

"So, what you going to do now? Let me go or kill me, pet dog?"

"Stand up." Sandi stood up.

"Now what?"

"Turn around." When she turned around, Trayvon knocked her out cold with the butt of the gun. He watched as her body hit the floor. He picked up the bag that was on her bed and walked out of the room, knowing what he had to do. He walked into the kitchen and turned the gas on high, lit a candle she had on the kitchen table and walked out of the house. Within five minutes, the house exploded into full flames. He started his car and drove off. He had to make it look like an accident he didn't need no more police looking into another homicide.

Chapter 9

Porscha walked into the apartment and right up to her stash spot where she cooked up all the work. Corey looked at her as she walked into the apartment, and he walked up to her.

"Everything is ready like I told you it would be. I have four kilos broke down into grams already bagged up, and I have twenty kilos already in six duffle bags, ten kilos in each bag ready to be shipped out."

"Good, that's what I like to see. Have the workers clean this place up, we are moving locations. Make sure this place is ready to go by tomorrow morning. I'm sending Terry over to make the pickups."

"Is there a reason why we moving locations?"

"Yeah, I just had a not so friendly meeting with Mannino, so I just want to be ready for whatever."

"Cool. I'll have some more guys come over just to be on the safe side."

"Do that and keep me posted." Porscha looked around one more time before walking off.

***

"Domenico, I want you to find out everything on that nigga Porscha. It's time to show her who really runs Manhattan. This bitch want war, let's give her war,"

Mannino said as he was sitting at the bar taking shots of gin back-to-back.

"I'll take care of it for you, Mannino, but what I do know so far is that one of her headquarters is in Stuy Town. Some of the guys been keeping an eye out over there for me." Mannino lowered his head and lit his cigar.

"Let it be known if you see any of these niggas, shoot on sight. I'm done talking." Mannino picked up his drink, took a shot and nodded at Domenico, as Domenico walked off to go stand on the business.

***

The black-on-black Cadillac Escalade platinum edition pulled up on the docks. There were workers unloading the cargo units. Porscha's driver opened the back door for her to step out. Porscha and her two men walked to where the cargo unit was with all the weapons. Porscha looked down at all the M16s, AR-15s, MAC-11s, P90s, Glock-9s, 9MMs and much more. She smiled and shook her head.

"Damn, Porscha, we can supply a small army with all this shit."

"Yeah, we can. Rakim, get everything in the vans so we can start moving them out of here. I don't want to be here a minute longer than I have to. I'm going to go check on the girls." Porscha walked off as Rakim nodded his head at her and called a few guys over to him. Porscha walked to the last cargo unit. She looked at Estabon's two men standing there. She nodded at them, that's when they opened the unit up. Porscha covered her nose up from the smell on the inside coming out.

Estabon's men yelled out, "Come out now. Line up, side by side, no talking." Porscha looked at all the females they couldn't be more than twenty-five years old. They were all beautiful. She walked in front of all of them and counted them all one by one, then she looked at Estabon's men as she walked over to them.

"Estabon said there would be twenty females. I only count eighteen. I'm missing two girls." Both men looked at each other then. Inside the cargo container towards the back there were two dead females laying on the floor.

One of Estabon's men said, "There are your other two females inside, dead."

"And what the fuck am I going to do with two dead females?"

"Don't worry about it, we will take care of it on the way back, shark food." Porscha pulled her phone out as she walked off to call Trayvon. After a few seconds, he picked up.

"Hey, how is everything going down there?"

"We have a problem." Trayvon placed District Attorney Smith's papers down that he was reading over before talking.

"And what is this problem?"

"There is only eighteen out of twenty. The trip was too long for two of them, they ain't make it." Trayvon placed his finger on his head and closed his eyes for a second before talking.

"That's not on us, just take care of everything else and I'll make the phone call to our friend."

"Ok."

"I'll call you when I talk to him."

"Ok." Porscha hung up the phone and walked back to Estabon's men.

"Everything is taken care of. I'll take it from here." She turned around and looked at all the girls.

"Follow me." She walked them to a U-Haul truck where they got inside. Her man closed the door as she walked over to Rakim.

"You ready? I'm trying to get off this fucking dock now."

"Yeah, I have everything loaded up."

"Good, go to the warehouse. Corey should already be there. I have to go to Club Mercedes to drop these girls off to Paris. I'll get up with you tomorrow."

"Say less, I'll see you tomorrow." Porscha walked off as she pulled her phone out to call Paris.

***

"Detective Flowers, you have a minute before you leave for the night?"

"Yeah, Boatwrite, what's up?" Detective Flowers stopped to talk to her.

"Did you know there was a house fire tonight on Overland Avenue?"

"No, I been so wrapped up in trying to find out who this mystery girl is, I haven't been paying attention to nothing else. What about this fire?"

"Ready for this? It was District Attorney Sandi Smith's house, sister to Judge John Smith."

"And her house was on fire?"

"Yeah, it burned down to the ground with her inside of it. What you think about that?"

"I'm thinking foul play. How did the fire start?"

"She left the gas on in the house. That caused the explosion, what is the odds of that?"

"You know what, Boatwrite? I'm telling you this female is bigger than we know, whoever she is. She is the shot caller making all the plays."

"Then we need to hurry up and find out who she is, before New York City becomes body land."

"First thing in the morning, let's tag team this then."

"You got it, Boatwrite." Detective Flowers walked off, knowing that this female was someone not to be fucked with.

Chapter 10

There were two vans parked outside of the StuyTown Apartments, unloading boxes. People were walking around and sitting on the benches outside the apartments. Corey came walking out with a few guys laughing and joking, not paying attention to the two white vans. That's when one of the Italian men nodded at the other one and they pulled out two M16s and started shooting at all of them. Everyone heard gunshots and people screaming as bullets were flying. Corey pulled his gun out and started shooting back as he was running for cover. Two of his guys were gunned down, along with a few other people. Corey was shooting from behind a tree at both vans as bullets were flying his way.

"Fuck! Where the hell did these noodle eating motherfuckers come from?" he asked himself. Corey came from behind the tree and saw and heard both vans peeling and speeding off. He looked around at all the dead people and his two men laying in pools of blood, along with people who were shot. There was broken glass from the windows that were shot out. He heard the police siren coming his way. He tucked his gun away and put his hoodie on and walked to his car. He got in and pulled off before the police arrived.

***

Rakim walked to the back of the warehouse as he talked on the phone with Corey.

"What the fuck went down?"

"I don't know where the fuck these fat fucks came from, but they wasn't doing no talking, they came out blasting. They bodied two of the homies and like six other motherfuckers."

"Fuck, is everything out the spot?"

"Yeah, that place is cleaned out, Porscha had us do it last night. I was turning the keys in when they pulled up clapping."

"Stay low, let me call Porscha and let her know what just popped off."

"Copy that." Rakim hung up the phone, knowing it was time to get activated. Porscha wasn't going to have no understanding for this shit.

***

Porscha looked around the club, the females were all dressed up looking their best, Paris had made sure they had the best of everything. Porscha walked up to Paris.

"They look outstanding. Remember, each girl needs to bring no less than fifteen hundred in tonight. I don't want no excuses out of none of them, we all have a part to play, no matter how much we dislike it."

"They know, I told them already, and Terry brought me the other package this morning."

"Then you need to start getting to the bag, you have a lot on your plate now." Porscha stopped talking when her phone went off. She saw it was Rakim calling her, so she walked off to answer the phone out of everyone's hearing. Paris knew something was wrong by Porscha's body language.

***

"Look at this fucking place, it looks like World War 3 out here. Eight dead people, windows shot out, can someone tell

50

me what the fuck happened?" Captain Lawson asked as he looked around the scene.

"I talked to a few people. Witnesses are saying two vans was parked over there in those parking spaces, and two heavyset Italians with two skinny Italians, was shooting some high-power weapons at a few Black dudes coming out the apartments," Detective Flowers said.

"So, we have a Black and Italian turf war going on."

"Sir, two days ago there was a meeting with Mannino Caporegime and our mystery woman. It didn't go so friendly. This might be a blow back from Roberto Reddinger's murder."

"What about our FBI friends, Agent Stallone and Agent Sampaio, what do they have to say about this?"

"They are talking with the senior chief of the FBI agency about all of this, sir, to see if they can ID her."

"Get me a full report on my desk and I'll make some calls to see what strings I can pull on this fucking nightmare."

"Ok, Captain."

"Where is Detective Boatwrite?"

"She's looking into District Attorney Sandi Smith's house fire."

"Yeah, because I ain't going for a pot on and she didn't remember she left it on. That sounds like some bullshit to me."

"Boatwrite's not going for it either, sir."

"Ok, keep me posted on everything."

"Will do."

***

Trayvon walked into the private restaurant, headed to the back table where Attorney Chris Smith, Judge Adam Miller and Mayor Micheal Rapkin were talking, waiting on him to show up Trayvon walked up to the table and sat down.

"Gentlemen… gentlemen, how is it going?" Trayvon asked with a smile on his face.

"If it isn't the man of the hour," Judge Miller said.

"There is something I would like to show you, Trayvon. This just came across my table last night, you may need to take a look at it," Mayor Rapkin said as he passed Trayvon a file. Trayvon opened the file and was looking at pictures of Porscha and Rakim having a meeting with Mannino Caporegime, Trayvon placed the file down on the table.

"So, what now?"

"The senior chief of the FBI is a personal friend of mine. He knows all about you and your daughter, so when it came to him, he brought it to me. I told him what you do for all of us. So, he shut down their investigation before it could start, but there is one problem. They are still working on the Paul Ross case and that may pull your daughter Porscha into the case. That's why I asked Chris to be here today with us."

"Trayvon, I will protect your daughter, they won't touch her. I'm the best at what I do." Trayvon nodded as he pulled out a cigar and lit it before talking.

"Chris, I appreciate that, I really do, but there won't be no investigation. When you play with fire, you get burned. Rapkin, how much is this gone to cost me to make this go away?" Trayvon puffed on his cigar

"Trayvon, what you mean, go away?"

"To kill the problem, Rapkin."

"Trayvon, you are talking about killing FBI agents."

"It won't be the first time, give me a number, Mayor." Mayor Rapkin took a deep breath before talking, shaking his head.

"A million dollars, five hundred grand apiece for the both of them, that's what it's going to cost for you to kill both of them."

"Done." Trayvon looked at everyone at the table when he said that.

"Trayvon, at no time do you need to be seen with your daughter. As of right now, she is the boss of the Medellin Cartel in New York. She don't have your last name, there's nothing that can tie y'all together. If you are seen with her, you lose this seat at the table with us."

Trayvon nodded after what Judge Miller said to him.

"Trayvon, remember you are the puppet master, and your daughter is the puppet. You pull the strings to make her move."

"I know, Mayor Rapkin."

"Good, now let's order. I'm losing weight over here." Trayvon puffed on his cigar again in deep thought.

Chapter 11

"So, this fat fuck thinks I'm someone to play with? Let me tell y'all something. On my way over here, I passed the graveyard and it's still room in there for them noodle eating pasta motherfuckers. Strap up, it's time to pop the mother fucking bottle."

"Porscha, you want to do this right now? It's still hot out there, police is everywhere."

"Did you not hear me? When I said strap the fuck up, get ready, nigga! Shit is about to go boom! Them pasta eating motherfuckers just opened up Pandora's Box, so congrats to them. Now they are in the belly of the fucking beast."

***

Mannino sat at the table eating with Domenico, outside of his restaurant, along with five of his bodyguards as they talked.

"The job was taken care of, Mannino. Porscha will get the message of who the fuck she is dealing with."

"How many people were killed?"

"Over five. Trust me, she got the message."

"I want her fucking dead, and everything around her."

"We are working on all that right now, Mannino. Her body will be in the East River real soon." Mannino nodded as he was eating.

***

Porscha sat in the back seat of the supercharged Suburban Tahoe with a fully loaded P90 in her hand. She had three supercharged Suburban Tahoes riding down Main Street, one in front of the other. Every one of her shooters was holding a high-powered assault rifle with a switch. Everyone had Murder One masks over their faces, they were all ready to kill anyone who was at the restaurant. Porscha's phone went off, she saw it was her father calling her.

"Hey." Porscha pulled her mask off as she talked to her father.

"Porscha, listen to me. You have two FBI agents following you. They are trying to build a case against you. The meeting you had with Mannino, they were there. I'm going to send you their picture, so you know what they look like. Watch how you move out there."

"I got you, Father. I'm going to take care of something right now and I'll look into those FBI agents."

"Ok, be safe. I love you."

"I love you more, Daddy." Porscha hung up the phone. That's when the pictures came through. She looked at both of them and thought back at the one person that was looking at her at the restaurant, the day of the meeting with Mannino Caporegime.

"Porscha, we are about to be at the restaurant."

"Good, let's light this bitch up." Porscha put her Murder One mask on and cocked her P90 back.

Mannino looked up and that's when all he saw was the guns out the windows of the Suburban Tahoes. As he went to run, bullets were flying his way. He fell to the ground as all three Suburban Tahoes stopped in front of the restaurant. All the doors opened up, bullets were flying everywhere. Three of Mannino's men were hit. Mannino went to run into the restaurant and was shot in the back. Domenico went to pull his gun out and was shot in the arm and shoulder, the impact of the blast made him fly through the window. It was an all-out shootout on Main Street. Mannino's men were firing back at Porscha and her guys. Mannino made it inside the restaurant, he was laying on the floor behind a table bleeding out. Broken glass was flying everywhere. People were screaming, running for cover. Everyone heard police sirens coming their way.

Porscha looked and saw two police cars headed right at her. Rakim pointed the M16 at the police cars and started firing at them. Corey did the same thing, but Corey hit the officer driving, making him crash into the other police car, flipping it over. Rakim was still shooting at the police car as it was on its back, hitting the gas tank, and making it explode. Bursting into flames and killing the two cops. Porscha looked and noticed Detective Boatwrite and FBI Agent Stallone getting out of the other cop car. She started shooting at them as she was walking towards them. FBI Agent Stallone went to help Detective Boatwrite up when one of Porscha bullets hit him in the back. He turned around from the impact, that's when Porscha shot him five more times in the chest, killing him. Detective Boatwrite just looked at his body hit the ground as blood just came out of his mouth. She ran behind her car.

Porscha's men were still shooting up the restaurant. Porscha looked and saw two of her guys dead in the streets. She also saw more police cars headed their way, and she yelled out, "Get their bodies in the trucks we have to go now." As they were putting their bodies in the SUVs, Porscha, Rakim, and Corey were still shooting at the other cop cars, making them stop. They all got into the SUVs as the drivers pulled off, still shooting from the windows at the restaurant until they were out of sight.

"Get to the spot right now, we have to get off the streets with these SUVs now," Porscha said as she took her mask off.

Chapter 12

Captain Lawson and the senior chief of the FBI, along with forty more cops and FBI agents were on the scene. It was a madhouse on Main Street. Two local news teams were on the scene shooting live. There was five dead Italians, two dead police officers and one dead FBI agent. Six people were shot inside the restaurant, which was destroyed. Mannino and Domenico was taken out the back of the restaurant by Mannino's men before the police arrived. There were over four thousand bullet cases on the ground. Cars that were parked on the streets were shot up, their windows shot out of them. Police cars were flipped over. CSI was on the scene and people were standing around, looking. Captain Lawson walked up to the senior chief of the FBI, Goldwyn.

"What a fucking mess out here, this looks worse than World War 2."

Senior Chief Henry Goldwyn looked at Captain Lawson.

"One of my agents is dead, laying under a white sheet because they didn't follow a direct order, after I told them they do not have authorization to work on this case. Look at this shit show somebody's ass is on the line. The press is going to have a ball with this."

"This is a turf war, Goldwyn. This is payback from the StuyTown shooting and we ain't even in the eye of the storm yet."

"And why you say that?"

"Because witnesses to the shooting said that Mannino Caporegime was shot here today. The shooters were after him, he may even be dead."

"We might not be in the eye of the storm, but this is what I do know, and you should know it too, Captain. Until that body shows up, Mannino Caporegime ain't dead." Captain Lawson nodded his head, knowing Senior Chief Goldwyn was right. He looked and saw Detective Boatwrite talking with Detective Flowers and FBI Agent Sampaio a little way up.

"Boatwrite, what happened out here today?" Detective Flowers asked her.

"I don't fucking know, it all happened so fast. We heard over the radio there was a shooting on Main Street. As we were coming to the scene, someone started shooting at us. Next thing I know, the car was flipping over. The other police car exploded, bursting into flames, Agent Stallone got out of the car, he went to help me out, that's when I saw him get shot. His body jerked then he hit the ground."

"Do you think you can ID the shooter?" Detective Flowers said.

"No, all of them were covered up dressed in all-black, but what I do know the one who shot Agent Stallone was a female. I could tell because of her body shape. I know it was a female." Agent Sampaio looked at Detective Flowers.

"My gut is telling me this is the same female shooter who killed Roberto Reddinger and the same female we saw having the meeting with Mannino."

"We need to find out who the fuck she is, because shit just got real," Detective Boatwrite said as she looked around at the scene.

***

Porscha walked to the bar in her office and poured herself a shot of Ciróc. She shook her head and brought the whole bottle back to her desk. She sat down and as she poured another shot there was a knock at the door, Porscha yelled, "Come in." That's when Rakim walked into her office. He looked at her drinking and walked to the bar and picked up a shot glass, then walked over to her desk and sat down in front of it as she poured him a shot of Ciróc.

"It was crazy out there today, Porscha. A lot of people got bodied. Innocent people that had nothing to do with anything got put to rest today."

"Anybody that was at Mannino's restaurant wasn't innocent. You know what I call that? Collateral damage. I had a point to prove. There are no innocent people, everybody is guilty of something."

"So, what now?"

"We take shit over. Terry has Castle Hill, Corey has Polo Grounds Towers, Lance got Patterson Houses, you have Brownsville Houses and Paris is running Club Mercedes. We are making two million a week and I'm not going to let nobody fuck that up. So today, we had to stand on business to let everyone know Pandora's Box can open or stay closed, and shit can go boom real fast."

"It's two dead cops and one dead FBI agent. It's all over the news."

Porscha took a sip of her Ciróc before talking. "I know. I made sure I killed the FBI agent that was following us. He was trying to open up an investigation, so I made sure I put all that shit to rest. The Tahoes, where are they?"

"Crashed all three of them. I made sure that was done personally, that's why I'm just now getting back."

"Ok, make sure everyone is on point, because one thing I do know, Mannino is going to strike back hard."

"I'm going to go take care of that right now."

Porscha just nodded as Rakim got up and walked out of her office. She took another shot and turned the news on.

***

It was 9:55 pm. Trayvon was dressed in all-black. He was in the back of the warehouse hiding in the bushes. He'd been there since 8:30 pm because he wanted to know who District Attorney Smith was coming to meet. That's when he saw a shadow walking his way. He waited until he was in the back of the warehouse before he came out of the bushes, gun pointed at him. When he saw Trayvon and the gun pointed at his head, he just put his hands in the air.

"Who the fuck are you?" Trayvon asked as he walked closer to him.

"Brad Smith and who the fuck are you?" Trayvon walked up on him so he could see his face.

"I let your family go. I kept my end of the deal, and you are still coming at me?"

"Where is my sister?"

"She dead, because of you."

"Bullshit, she dead because of monsters like you."

"Before she died, she told me everything. That's how I knew to meet you here tonight."

"So, what… you going to kill me now?"

"No, I have my peoples going to get your wife and kids. I'm going to set them on fire in front of you, then I'm going to kill you so you will know how you fucked up."

"You don't have to do that. I have nothing on you or nobody else. She was going to bring it to me tonight. The last time we met here, it was just so she can see me, that's all." Trayvon thought about what he said. The bag he took from Sandi had all of the evidence inside, so he knew he was telling the truth.

"I believe you."

"So, are you going to let me live?"

"No." Trayvon pulled the trigger, killing Brad Smith. He shot him two times in the head. He took his phone from him and his ID. As much as he hated it, he knew he had to kill District Attorney Shawn Croughton and his family, along with Judge Brad Smith's family. They became a liability to him and his daughter. Trayvon went and got his Ford VelociRaptor 600 horsepower pickup truck and pulled it to the back of the warehouse. He pulled the tarp out and wrapped Judge Smith's body up in it and tied it up with rope. He placed his body on the back of the pickup truck and drove him to the water, where he tied him down with bricks and dragged his body inside the water, before getting back in his truck driving off.

Chapter 13

Mannino stood up by the window smoking his cigar, his left shoulder was wrapped up in a sling. He couldn't believe he was almost killed, he thought he was going to die when he got shot. He'd lost a lot of blood. Domenico was still fighting for his life and the doctor said Domenico's situation was touch and go. He had a sixty to forty percent chance of living. Out of thirty years in the mafia, he never was caught slipping like this. He turned around when he heard a knock at the door.

"Come in." The door opened and he saw Tony come into his office, along with Big Pate.

"How you feeling, Mannino?" Tony asked.

"How the fuck you think I feel? Beside this fucking hole in my shoulder, I'm fucking great. What y'all got to tell me?"

"It's ugly out there, Mannino. Right now, the pigs are everywhere, the restaurant is shot to shit. The police have it marked off as a crime scene, we can't even get in there. We lost five guys and a few innocent people that was eating at the restaurant was killed. Plus, two dead police officers and one dead FBI agent, it's ugly, Mannino."

Mannino puffed on his cigar before talking.

"I want to know everything about this nigga. Where she sleeps, eats, fucks. Send everyone at her. I want her fucking dead! Do you hear me, dead."

That's when there was another knock at the door. Tony walked and opened the door. Joey was standing there.

"What is it?" Mannino asked as he puffed on his cigar.

"You have two detectives downstairs here to talk with you."

Mannino looked at Tony and Big Pate and nodded as he walked out the door headed downstairs.

***

Trayvon sipped on his Hennessy and smoked his cigar as the private Stratos 716X jet was landing in Colombia. He took the last shot of his Hennessy before stepping off the plane. Estabon Sanchez had the Mercedes-Benz Brabus G550 4X4 picking him up. Trayvon placed both suitcases in the Benz Brabus and sat in the back seat and puffed on his cigar as he headed to Estabon's home. It took the driver twenty-five minutes to get to Estabon's thirty-million-dollar mansion. Trayvon looked around at all the guards dressed in black and green, holding assault rifles. Estabon had his own military army at his mansion. The driver stopped the Benz Brabus and opened the doors for Trayvon to step out. Estabon smiled as he walked up to Trayvon. Trayvon smiled back as they shook each other's hands.

"Trayvon, it's good to see you again. Come, come... let's walk and talk."

"It's good to see you again too, Estabon. You have fourteen million dollars in the two suitcases in the G-wagon. I counted it twice personally myself."

"You are an honest man. I like that about you." Trayvon couldn't believe how nice his house was.

"You have a beautiful home, Estabon."

"Thank you, it took five years to build it."

"So, tell me why you had me fly out to your beautiful country?"

"Just a report to look into your eyes. How is business going in America?" Estabon pulled out his cigar and lit it as Trayvon talked.

"It's only been four months, so we are still taking over turfs as we plant our flag. My daughter Porscha is running the cartel while I deal with politics and politicians. the judges, district attorneys, the mayor of New York, there are a lot of people I have to pay off to look the other way. So when it comes to the cartel, I'm a ghost. But when it comes to the politics and politicians, I am actively involved. So, we both have our jobs to do and we are doing very well."

"I understand, but it's been a lot of murders and police killings. Is that not bad for business in New York City?"

"Respectfully Estabon, name one cartel who ain't kill a few people on its way to greatness. Sometimes murder is a must, the only language people understand."

"You are right, many people died for the rise of the Medellin Cartel, Trayvon."

"My daughter is making plans big plans to take New York City by storm."

"So, she can move a larger amount of cocaine?"

"Let me call her and see when she would be ready."

"Ok, but we can do that later. Come, let's eat and drink now, we talk about business later."

***

Mannino walked downstairs where Detective Boatwrite and Detective Flowers were waiting on him. He looked at both of them as he pulled on his cigar.

"Mannino Caporegime, thank you for seeing us. I'm Detective Boatwrite and this is my partner, Detective Flowers."

"No problem, what can I do for you?"

"Yesterday, your restaurant was shot up and five people were killed outside of the restaurant. On the inside, three more people were killed and more wounded by gunshots. And there's been reports that you were shot as well, but there was no police report made about the shooting at the restaurant. Why is that?"

"My manager was down there at the time of the shooting, and he did make a police report out. As you can see, I am not shot at all. I wasn't there at the time of the shooting." Detective Flowers shook his head.

"Look, Mannino, you are dealing with some real heavy hitters. This female already had three cops killed, one was an FBI agent. She's not playing now. We are here to help you out, so you can live another day. So, you can either play ball with us or get killed because she is winning right now." Mannino puffed on his cigar before talking.

"Detectives, thanks for dropping by. Pate, get the door for them."

"Have it your way. We don't mind investigating your murder because we will already know who ordered your hit." Mannino watched as both detectives walked out the door, he then looked at Big Tony.

"Find this bitch and kill her." He then walked off, headed back upstairs to put his sling back on. His arm was killing him, but he had to play it off for the police.

* * *

Porscha looked at all the weapons Estebon sent for her to sell. It was six hundred assault rifles at a thousand apiece. She had to think long and hard about selling them, knowing she was at war. She was at her new warehouse in Manhattan, she had all the guns, drugs, and money there. Fifteen guards walked around with assault rifles. The warehouse had three floors. On the first floor was a high-end winery, where the best wine was sold. The second floor was where they made the wine, she called it Porscha Winery. The basement is where she had the cocaine broken down and cooked up, along with the money counted up. There was a secret door that you had to take to get to the basement that Porscha had well hidden, and only fifteen workers down there. Five to cook up and make the kilos and bag up the grams, five to count the money up, and five to keep inventory and the books. She walked up to Corey as he was smoking a blunt, watching the workers.

"You know a lot more bodies are going to drop before this is over, right?"

"I know, it's just… this is crazy, we are going toe to toe with the mafia, the Jamaican Hitters tucked they tails when they seen how we pulled up blasting. now we got them pushing our weight and we ain't even have to take over the projects, shit, the niggas everyone was buying from started buying from us. Shit, we even got niggas from Brick City, Jersey, coming 'cross that water buying from us."

"This is just the start of my takeover. We just got to keep standing on our business, that's all."

"Yeah, but we killing cops and FBI agents. We don't need that type of heat on us."

"Trust me, I have a plan for that too. We will never see the inside of a courtroom. Look, I have some things to go take care of, you got this down here?"

"Yeah, I got this, Porscha."

"Cool, I'll call you later." Porscha looked around one more time before leaving the warehouse. Her driver opened the door to her Rolls-Royce Cullinan for her to step inside. Once she got inside and pulled out her phone, not even ten minutes of driving through Manhattan, her car was pulled over.

"Porscha, two detectives just pulled us over."

"Let's see what New York's Finest have to say to us then."

Detective Boatwrite and Detective Flowers walked up to Porscha's car door and knocked on the window. Porscha rolled down the window and looked at them.

"I'm not driving, so is there a reason you are at my window?"

"We need you to step out of the car." Porscha smiled as she stepped out of the car.

"Now what, Detective? Because everything you are doing right now is illegal and trust me, I know my rights and I have an attorney that costs two thousand dollars an hour."

"I just want to look into the eyes of the female who had a good cop killed, and a lot of other innocent people killed," Detective Boatwrite said as she looked into Porscha's eyes.

"You know, Detective, you said a good cop was killed and a lot of innocent people, but you know what? Everyone is guilty of something and FYI, I had nobody killed. Now, if we are done here, I have things to do."

"I'll see you around, and just know when I do put them cuffs on you, they are going to be FBI Agent Stallone's cuffs since he was killed in your shootout yesterday."

"Have a nice day, Detective, your boss will get a call from my attorney in the morning." Porscha smiled as she got back into her car and her driver pulled off.

"Boatwrite, you know we are going to hear about this in the morning."

"You know what, Flowers? At this point, I really don't give a fuck."

Detective Boatwrite grilled Porscha's car as it pulled off.

Chapter 14

Trayvon woke up to the sun's rays on his face. He opened his eyes to two beautiful females standing in front of his bed naked. Both females were a little darker than yellow. One of them had long, jet-black hair and green eyes. She had an hourglass body, with tattoos on her thighs and stomach. The other female had long blonde hair with hazy eyes, with tattoos just over her breasts. Her body was just like Beyonce's. Trayvon sat up in the bed and looked at both females.

"Mr. Sanchez told us to come wake you up, breakfast will be ready in an hour."

"I love the way you woke me up."

"Then you are going to love this even more." Both females climbed in the bed with Trayvon and pulled the covers back, as one of the females pulled his boxers off. She smiled when she saw his thick manhood. She took her hand and rubbed over his abs as she was sucking on his manhood. While the other female was kissing him, Trayvon closed his eyes as he felt the wetness of the one female's hot box sliding down his manhood, he grabbed her hips. As she was riding him, the other female placed her legs over his face as her pussy found his tongue. She was moving her hips in a circular motion as her hands were on his chest.

"Damn, papi, I can feel you in my stomach. You have good dick, daddy."

She started riding his dick harder and harder as she was cumming all over his manhood.

"My turn, I want some dick too." Both females switched positions. Trayvon could hold it no longer, so he grabbed her hips as he started to cum deep inside of her.

"Damn, papi, I felt that load." Both females started laughing as they got up off Trayvon and took his hand as they walked him to the shower.

***

Captain Lawson hung up his phone and walked to his office doors and yelled out in an angry voice, "Detective Boatwrite and Detective Flowers, my office, now." Both detectives looked at each other.

"Come on, Boatwrite, it's time to hear the bullshit."

"Like I told you yesterday, I'm at the point where I don't give a fuck." Both detectives walked into Captain Lawson's office. He grilled them both.

"Close my door and have a seat now." They both sat down in front of the captain's desk.

"For the last hour, I was on a conference call with Mayor Rapkin, Senior Chief Goldwyn from the FBI and our own chief of police, along with Attorney Chris Salini. Let me jump headfirst into this, do you know who you pulled over yesterday?"

"No sir, we just know she is a big wig in the city, and she is the new shot caller," Detective Boatwrite said.

"Let me tell you who she is. Her name is Porscha Shields, her ties run deeper than you know. FBI Agent Sampaic is suspended without pay for working an investigation on Porscha Shields. An investigation that caused his partner, FBI Agent Stallone to be killed after Senior Chief Goldwyn told them they do not have authorization to work the investigation."

"Just because she has deep ties, we are going to let a cop killer go free?" Detective Flowers asked.

"What proof do you have that she is a cop killer, Detective?"

"Captain, over the last four or five months, rumors that District Attorney Shawn Croughton and his family, along with Judge Brad Smith and his family were all kidnapped. To put icing on the cake, the star witness FBI Agent Paul Ross, who was working on the case, was shot in the head and his body set on fire. That happened the day before Emilio Sanchez's court day for killing his uncle, cartel boss Juanito Sanchez.

"Let me remind you, Emilio Sanchez was arrested under a fake name—Alverez Sliver. Now this is where all fingers start pointing at Porscha Shields. Someone moved in on Roberto Reddinger's turf. Porscha Shields had a meeting with Robert Reddinger. We know this because when we were investigating the murder video footage of them two having a meeting, not even a week later, he was gunned down on Main Street with two of his bodyguards. The shooter was a female dressed in all-pink. The same day, Rude Boy and four of his men got killed and someone took over his turf.

"FBI Agent Stallone and I were following Mannino Caporegime. He went to Per Se five-star restaurant and guess who showed up to have a meeting with him? Porscha Shields. Two days later, StuyTown Apartments get shot up, witnesses say it was a few Italian guys shooting high power weapons at some black guys. Now, StuyTown used to be Roberto Reddinger's turf, and the blow back in three SUVs pulled up in front of Mannino Caporegime restaurant and all hell breaks loose. Two police officers and one FBI agent gets killed by the shooters in the SUVs, and one of the shooters was a female. Matter of fact, the shooter that killed Agent Stallone was a female, Captain," Detective Flowers said.

"Detective Flowers, I hear what you are saying, but not one thing you said is proof that Porscha is the shot caller or a cop killer. Detective Flowers, you as well as Detective Boatwrite, are off the case. I'm saying this now and I'm going to make it real clear. If I get wind that you two are working this case, you both will be suspended without pay."

"Captain—"

"Detectives, have a good day."

"Captain Lawson—"

"I said, have a good day, Detectives." Both detectives got up and walked out of the office without saying another word. Once out of the captain's office, Detective Boatwrite looked at Flowers.

"What the fuck was that about all in there?" Detective Boatwrite asked.

"Money. Whoever Porscha is and whoever is backing her up, their money is too long, and they are too powerful. We've just seen that."

Detective Boatwrite shook her head and walked off.

***

Trayvon walked up to the table where Estabon was seated.

"Please have a seat, Trayvon, and have some of the broccoli cheddar pasta bake. Trust me, it is to die for."

"Sure, I'll have some then."

"How are you feeling this morning, Trayvon?"

"The way your females woke me up, I'm feeling outstanding."

'Good, I'm glad to hear that. Now, let's talk business, shall we?"

"Yes, let's talk business."

"I want to up the supply from eighteen hundred kilos a month to forty-five hundred a month, and if you can do this, I'll lower the price of every kilo to say… twenty thousand. How does that sound?"

"If I say yes, what will be the time frame to pay you back?"

"How does ninety days sound?"

"It sounds fair. Let's do this, we will do two shipments at forty-five hundred kilos. Let's see how they move. Then, if everything goes right, we keep it at that number."

"That sounds good to me. Now, let's eat. You are going to love this food."

"Estabon, where is your son? I haven't seen him since my first trip to your country."

"He is in Mexico, having a sit-down with the Sinaloa Cartel. He will be back in a few days."

"Give him my best wishes when you talk with him."

"I will."

Chapter 15

Lucchese Bonanno's car pulled up in front of Mannino Caporegime's house. Lucchese and three of his men walked to the front door, where Mannino's guard opened the door for them to come inside. Lucchese walked up to Mannino and gave him a hug and kiss on the cheek. "How are you feeling Mannino?"

"I'm living. I would be doing a lot better when I kill this mix breed bitch."

"Yeah, that's what I came to talk to you about."

"Come, Lucchese, let's go out back and talk, and share a cigar and tell me what's on your mind." Both men went out back to talk.

"Mannino, I'm going to cut right to the point. You are making the other families look bad here, and that's not good for no one."

"I have my peoples looking for her right now, so I can skin that bitch alive."

"Mannino, I'm telling you this one time, take care of this problem. For years now, you been moving sloppy, and it don't look good on the rest of the families. So, you handle this before this problem handles you."

"I'm on it, Lucchese, you have my word."

"Good. Now, come on, we got the guys in the house." Lucchese patted Mannino on the arm as they walked inside.

***

"Rakim, I'm on my way to you now. I'm just getting into the Escalade now. I'll be there in twenty minutes tops. Just make sure you have everyone on standby for their pickups and drop-offs."

"I already did that. Everybody's money is counted for already, the orders are already on standby, Porscha."

"Ok, I'll see you in a few minutes then." Porscha hung up the phone as she rode in the back seat of the Escalade. Her driver looked in the rearview mirror at the two Jeep Wrangler's riding behind them. He noticed they rolled their windows down and started pulling up on the side of them. That's when he noticed the guns.

"Porscha, get down, we are about to get hit." Porscha looked out the window and saw the assault rifles pointed at her Escalade. That's when they heard the sound of gunshots going off as bullets ripped through the Escalade, shooting the windows out and all. Porscha's driver was racing down the street as they were shooting the SUV up. He made a right down 45th Street. Porscha pulled her gun out and started shooting back at them. Bullets were flying everywhere, one of the Jeeps hit a car and flipped over on 45th Street.

Porscha's driver lost consciousness and hit a parked car. Porscha opened the back door and jumped out of the SUV. She was shooting at the driver of the Jeep when one of the passenger's bullets shot her in the shoulder. Porscha screamed as she still was shooting at Jeep coming her way. One of the bullets hit the driver in the head, making him turn the steering wheel, flipping the Jeep over. She ran out the way as it was coming her way. She ran up to the Jeep and shot both of Mannino's men in the head. She looked at the third man lying on the ground after he was thrown out the Jeep.

"Wait, wait, don't shoot me!"

"Why the fuck shouldn't I?" Porscha watched as he tried to grab his gun. She shot him in the arm, then in the leg. She walked up and smacked him in the back of the head with the gun, knocking him out cold. She looked around and ran to the front of the Escalade to her driver, who was dead in the front seat. She pushed his body to the passenger seat and got into the Escalade and backed it up.

She was bleeding badly. She took deep breaths as she opened up the back of the Escalade and cried out as she picked Mannino's man up. Once he was in the back of the Escalade, she closed the door and drove out of the dead-end street of the burned-down, abandoned warehouses. She pulled out her phone and called Rakim. After a few rings, Rakim picked up.

"Porscha, where are you, it's been forty-five minutes?"

With a deep breath, she responded, "I was shot. They tried to kill me."

"What you mean you were shot, where are you?"

"I'm about to be on Grand Avenue, come get me now. I can't drive no more." Porscha pulled over to the right and cut the Escalade off and closed her eyes as she passed out from loss of blood.

***

Detective Boatwrite looked around at the scene. Three of Mannino's guys was arrested on their way to the hospital from when the Jeep flipped over. Two dead men lay under white sheets. Detective Flowers walked up to Detective Boatwrite.

"So, here's what I got so far. Two black Jeeps was shooting at a gray Escalade. One of the Jeeps hit an oncoming car and flipped over, and the other Jeep kept on shooting at the Escalade. We found the other Jeep on the dead end of the abandoned warehouses, with two dead bodies in there, but we ain't find the gray Escalade."

"It's not hard to put two and two together. They were after Porscha. We find her, we find our gray Escalade," Detective Boatwrite said.

"You know we ain't on this case no more, right?"

"What are you talking about, Detective Flowers? We are investigating a shootout on 45th and Main we was called to." Detective Flowers smiled and walked off, knowing somehow this was going to blow back on them.

Chapter 16

Porscha opened her eyes. She was lying in a bed with an IV in her arm. Her eyesight was blurry, and she was weak. Her right arm was in so much pain from where she got shot at. She looked around the room not knowing where she was at. That's when Rakim walked into the room and looked at her with a smile on his face as he shook his head.

"What's up, Porscha, how you feeling?"

"Like a fucking truck hit me doing eighty miles an hour."

"Good, because it's good that you are in pain that means you can feel your body parts." Porscha closed her eyes before talking.

"How long I been here for?"

"Four days. You slept two days straight. You was in and out of it yesterday and today, you woke up."

"What happened, where did you pick me up at?"

"You were parked on Grant Avenue, I don't know how the police ain't see the Escalade shot up like that, but we got you here at my spot. Your driver, he ain't make it. You had one of them pasta eating motherfuckers in the back shot up. We patched him up and got him tied down right now. Somewhere real beautiful waiting on you."

"So, you put an IV in my arm?"

"Hell no. I called your father. He had the doctor come over here and do all of that. He knew your blood type and all already."

"So, where is my father now?"

"He was in Colombia, but when he found out what happened to you, he said he was on his way back." Before Porscha could say another word, the door opened up and Trayvon walked into the room. He looked at Rakim and walked up to Porscha and kissed her on the forehead as he held her hand.

"How are you feeling, baby?"

"I'm good, Dad."

"Porscha, I was worried about you. From here on out, I want a two-man detail with you from now on. Do I make myself clear?"

"Yes."

"Good. I agreed to forty-five hundred kilos for our next two shipments at twenty thousand a key. Can you move that?"

"Yeah, I can."

"Good, you don't have to worry about the police. I took care of that already. Porscha, you are a boss. I need you to start moving like one, ok?"

"Dad, I do."

"Bosses don't ride around with just their driver, because history shows us anybody can be killed. We are dealing with the cartel, so we have to start moving like them."

"Ok."

"Now it's time for you to strike back hard. You have to break his spirit, snatch his soul from his body. This has to be loud and messy to let New York City know you are not to be fucked with."

"I got this, Father."

"I know you do, now I have to go take care of some other business a few loose ends I need to tie up."

"Father, when you said don't worry about the police, what did you mean?"

"That FBI agent that was killed, that cost us half-a-million, but it's paid for, so it's dirt under the rug. Now, I have to go. I love you, baby girl."

"I love you more, Dad." Trayvon kissed her on the forehead before leaving the room. Porscha closed her eyes with hate in her heart, and Mannino was going to feel her pain like never before.

***

Mannino sat in his chair, smoking a cigar as Pete and Big Tony were talking to him in his office.

"So, what y'all both are telling me is that four of the guys are dead, three of them are locked up and one is missing, and we don't know if this bitch is dead or alive. That's what y'all are telling me, right?"

"Yeah, Mannino, that's what we are telling you," Pete said.

"You know this bitch has to have an angel watching over her. Ain't no way we can't kill her. Did you bail the guys out that were locked up?"

"Yeah, I sent Joey down there to get them out," Big Tony said.

"Look, it's hot right now. The police are everywhere, plus the other families are saying we are drawing too much attention from the police, and it's bad for business. So, we are going to let things cool down for a little while. Plus, I have my daughter's wedding this weekend and that's what I want to focus on."

"Whatever you say, Mannino," Pete said.

"Good, now let's go get some pasta. I'm fucking dying over here from hunger."

***

It was 8:30 pm when the two black on black, supercharged Suburban Tahoes pulled into the junkyard and drove all the way to the back. Rakim and Corey stepped out the Tahoes holding P90s with the switch in their hands. One of her bodyguards opened the door for her to step out the Tahoe. She walked up to Rakim and Corey as they walked up to the car compactor. Porscha walked up to the car compactor she looked at Mannino's man in her shot-up Cadillac Escalade, tied down to the front seat.

"I don't want to die like this, please, not like this. Get me out of here!" Mannino's man cried out in fear.

"Just think, the same Escalade you tried to kill me in, you are about to die in," Porscha said in a cold voice.

"Just shoot me in the head, please don't do this, not like this."

"You want to save your life, then you need to tell me something."

"What you want to know?" he asked with fear in his voice.

"Where does Mannino live?"

"I don't know."

"You are lying, crush him." They heard the car compactor crushing the Cadillac Escalade. The windows were breaking out and Mannino's man was screaming out of fear.

"Wait... wait... wait, I do know something." Porscha raised her hand in the air stopping them from crushing the Escalade.

"And what do you know?"

"Mannino's daughter is having a wedding this weekend in the Bronx, it's going to be big. It's going to be at Catholic Church. Mannino will be there, I swear to God."

"We'll see. Y'all can finish crushing the Escalade." The cries of Mannino's man and the crushing of the Escalade echoed and then they saw thick red blood coming out of the Escalade, on to the car compactor and ground. Porscha looked at Rakim.

"Get me the address to this Catholic Church."

"Will do."

"Now, let's get out of here. I need to check on the girls at Club Mercedes."

***

"Hey, Detective Flowers. You have a minute?" Detective Flowers looked at the officer walking his way, then at the time on the watch on his hand.

"Sure, what can I do for you, Officer?"

"Judge Brad Smith's wife, Jessica Smith, called and said her husband been missing for a week now."

"A week, why she ain't call after seventy-two hours? Did she say when was the last time she saw him?"

"She said he was on his way to see his sister, District Attorney Sandi Smith."

"And this was a week ago, right, Officer?"

"Yes, Detective."

"Something's not adding up because eight days ago, District Attorney Sandi Smith was killed in a house fire. That means Judge Brad Smith ain't know if he went to see her seven days ago. I need phone records. Let me get on this, thank you, Officer."

"No problem, Detective." Detective Flowers walked off, pulled his phone out and called Detective Boatwrite. After a few rings, she picked up.

"Hey, it's 9:45 pm, what do you want?" Detective Boatwrite said as she laid down.

"I need you to wake up. Guess who been missing for the last seven days?"

"I don't know, who?"

"Judge Brad Smith."

"Wait, Judge Brad Smith is missing?"

"Yeah, make sure you are down here first thing in the morning. We need to take a trip to see Judge Smith's wife."

"I'll be there." Detective Flowers hung up the phone and walked out of the police station.

***

Trayvon walked into the backyard. He was dressed in all-black. He had a black face mask on and black gloves. He picked the lock to the back door and walked into the house. He pulled his gun out and looked around downstairs to make sure no one was there, before walking upstairs step by step, gun in his hand. He pushed open the master bedroom door and saw Judge Smith's wife sleeping in the bed. He then walked out of the bedroom to the room down the hall and pushed the door open. Trayvon saw both of Judge Smith's daughters sleeping in the bed, they couldn't be more than ten years old. He took a deep breath and walked out of the room. In his heart he knew what he had to do, no matter how much he hated it. He closed his eyes, knowing this comes with cartel ties, he had to clean up all loose ends.

Chapter 17

Porscha was sitting down at the private restaurant eating lunch, when two black SUVs pulled up. Lucchese and four of his men stepped out of the SUVs and walked inside the restaurant, towards the back table where Porscha was. All Porscha's guards stood up and blocked their path.

Lucchese said, "I just came to talk to Porscha, you know a friendly lunch." One of Porscha's guards looked back at her. She nodded, letting him know to let him pass. Lucchese smiled as he walked up to Porscha.

"You mind if I have a seat?"

"No, please, sit down."

"You know I used to eat here all the time. The pasta is finger licking good, outstanding."

"So, you came here to tell me about the pasta?"

"No, I came to talk business with you, so we can get an understanding with each other."

"What type of business? I thought all you Italians wanted me dead."

"Hey, you always get one fucked up apple, out of a bucket of them. For God's sake, New York City is the rotten apple but killing you ain't come across our table yet. But it can be a topic depending on how this conversation goes, Porscha."

"So, cut to the chase, why are you here?"

"All business, I like that. This war that you and Mannino Caporegime have going on, it's fucking everyone's money up. And when my money start looking funny, then I come sit down and have a conversation with someone, and that someone is you." Porscha nodded.

"You know, I see history repeats itself, but I had this same conversation with Roberto, then Mannino, and now you… and we all were at a restaurant. Roberto was disrespectful to me and called me a shit eater, the pig. Mannino tried to get me to pay the price for being in Manhattan, so now I'm asking myself, what is it that you want out of me?"

"Let's help each other out, how's that sound? Let me lay my cards on the table." Lucchese put up five fingers and every time he said a New York City borough, he put one finger down. "Queens, Brooklyn, Staten Island, The Bronx, Manhattan. The mafia has a family in each one of them boroughs and together we are a closed fist, so here's the deal. We are giving you the green light to kill Mannino, he's been on our list. This is just icing on the cake from all his fuckups."

"If he's fucking up like that, why don't y'all just lay his ass to rest?"

"We all have rules to follow. Here's the thing, you killed over twelve Italians, all part of the mafia. So, you can kill him, or we can come together and kill you. It's fucked up, but hey, life is fucked up, Porscha."

"Y'all pasta eating motherfuckers are something else. So, what's in it for me? Because I'm not scared of war at all, we all bleed."

"You are right, we do all bleed, but let's make money together. How's that sound?"

"Good. I'm listening."

"How much weight can you provide us?"

"As much as you need, one hundred percent pure."

"Let's do this so we all can eat. Polo Grounds, Brownsville Houses, Patterson Houses, Castle Hill Houses, and Club Mercedes. The club and four projects are yours, don't sell out of them and my families will buy everything else off you to feed the rest of New York City. Everybody eats, everybody gets paid." Porscha thought for a second.

"I can do that."

"Good. Now, I have to go, but I'm telling you, Porscha... you should try that pasta, it's to die for."

"Maybe next time." Porscha got up and shook Lucchese's hand and followed up with a hug before he walked out the restaurant. She smiled, knowing that the mafia had been watching her. That reminded her to tighten up.

***

"I love Starbuck's Coffee, oh my God, it is so good," Detective Boatwrite said, as they were driving to Queens to see Judge Smith's wife.

"I don't get it. Why do you pay $10.00 for coffee? Ain't no way in hell," Detective Flowers said.

"Because you don't want the greater things in life. You are ok with a dollar and one cent coffee from the gas station that's been sitting all night."

"That's okay, I still have nine dollars, and ninety-nine cents left." They both started to laugh.

"That's the house right there to the right, Flowers, 1051 Bell Street."

"Yeah, let's see what she has to say. So, Boatwrite, do you think the rumors are true about them being kidnapped?"

"The man quit his job and moved his whole family within seventy-two hours, what you think?" Detective Boatwrite opened the car door and stepped out, along with Detective Flowers. They walked to the front door and knocked two times and rang the doorbell, but nobody came to the door. That's when the next-door neighbor came out the house and looked at both detectives.

"Hey is Mrs. Smith alright? She ain't bring the girls to school or go to work this morning. I knocked a few times on the door, but she ain't answer it." Both detectives shook their heads and pulled their guns out. They didn't say anything to the neighbor as they walked around the house, looking in the windows as they walked to the back of the house. Detective Boatwrite turned the knob on the door and opened it up. They went inside the house and upstairs, that's when Detective Boatwrite lowered her gun and shook her head as she looked at Detective Flowers.

"We have two bodies in here still in the bed."

"Yeah, and we have one more body in the bed in this room, Boatwrite."

"Come on, we have to call this in." Detective Boatwrite walked out of the house as she wiped away the tears from her eyes after looking at the two little girls shot dead in the bed. Within twenty minutes, the streets were blocked off, and twenty-plus officers were on the scene, along with CSI and two local news teams.

"Flowers, I want the sick motherfucker who did this."

"We are going to get them, I promise you that, Boatwrite. I promise you that."

***

Porscha walked into Club Mercedes and upstairs to her office, with all three of her bodyguards behind her. Paris walked into the office and up to Porscha.

"So, how are the girls working out?"

"All but one is making the quota." Porscha looked at her when she said that and shook her head.

"And why is that? We have a full house, nine hundred people came out to party and spend they money, so why ain't she making her quota?"

"She is still getting the hang of it."

"Bring her to me. Matter of fact, bring them all to me now."

"Some of them are on the floor now still working."

"Well, bring them to me now, so you should be moving getting them off the floor, Paris." Paris turned around and walked off. Within twenty minutes, she had all the girls in her office.

Looking at them, Porscha stood in front of them and said, "I don't like to repeat myself. I don't like having the same conversation twice, so let me make this real clear for the last time in front of all of y'all, so you understand where I'm coming from. Sandra, come here in front of all the ladies." Sandra walked up to Porscha in front of all the girls. She was young and beautiful. "Why haven't you been making your quota?"

"I have been trying, this is all still new to me." Porscha nodded.

"Paris, how much has Sandra made over the last two weeks?"

"Ten thousand dollars."

"So that means you are just dead weight here, because my bar alone makes forty thousand in a week. You are eleven thousand dollars short and that's bad for business. That means I don't need you." Paris closed her eyes, knowing what was about to happen, Porscha looked at one of her bodyguards and nodded, he grabbed Sandra and broke her neck in front of everyone, and then he let her body hit the floor. Porscha looked at everyone and said, "I don't want to have this conversation again. Sandra was useless, that means she was a waste. Paris, have her body wrapped up in plastic wrap and thrown in the trash dumpster, away from the club."

"Yes, Porscha."

"Ladies, now you can go back to the main floor, there is money down there waiting for y'all, so go get that money." All the girls walked out of the office. Porscha looked at Paris and walked up and said in her ear, "Next time this is on you. Tighten up, Paris. I'll send someone back for the last two weeks' drop-offs."

"Ok." Porscha put her glasses on her face and walked off.

Chapter 18

Trayvon stepped out of his car as he walked into the country club with a briefcase in his hand. He walked to the back room to the private VIP tables where Judge Adam Smith, Mayor Micheal Rapkin and to his surprise, FBI Senior Chief Henry Goldwyn were all seated at the table, smoking cigars and laughing with each other.

"Trayvon, come have a seat. We were just talking about you," Adam said.

"I hope it was all good things."

"Always, when it comes to your name. let me introduce you to FBI Senior Chief Henry Goldwyn." Trayvon reached his hand out to shake his.

"It's nice to finally meet you, Henry."

"Likewise, Trayvon, would you care for a cigar?"

"Sure." Henry passed the cigar to Trayvon.

"Have y'all seen the newspaper today?" Rapkin asked.

"Yeah, I read the front-page story, three killed in their home last night in Queens, mother and two daughters," Adam said.

"Yeah, on page two of the story it says Judge Brad Smith is missing and that it was his family that was killed. It also read on to say that his sister, District Attorney Sandi Smith, was killed in a house fire. What are the odds of all of this?" Henry added. Trayvon just puffed on his cigar as they talked, not saying a word.

"Trayvon, do you have any input on this conversation?"

"New York City is a very dangerous place. One should watch all the waters that they step in. I would like to show y'all all something." Trayvon placed the suitcase on the table and opened it up and passed everyone at the table a file to look over. Everyone at the table couldn't believe what they were reading.

"You have to be fucking kidding me," Adam said.

"Yeah, Sandi got all of that to Brad, so I had to go pay him a visit to make sure none of that got into the wrong hands."

"How did you know she got all of this to him?" Rapkin asked.

"Her cell phone. They were using burners, and I got my hands on hers, that's how I found his address and everything else."

"I can tell these are the original copies because they have the state seal, but how do we know he ain't make copies?"

"Mayor, trust me, he didn't. Y'all have my word on that."

"We take your word, Trayvon, but how do you know?"

"Because Adam, he's been missing for a week. I made sure I tied up all loose ends, so his family was, how do we say this… collateral damage for the safety of us at the table."

"Mayor Rapkin, Judge Miller, I like him. I fucking like him," Henry said as he looked at Trayvon.

***

Detective Boatwrite and Detective Flowers both walked into Captain Lawson's office and sat down in front of his desk. He looked at both of them and placed the newspaper down he was reading.

"Ok, I know why both of you are here. I talked to the chief this morning. Somebody is cleaning up some loose ends."

"Judge Smith's been missing for a week, matter of fact, a week and two days now. His sister was killed in a house fire, and I personally walked into the house and saw them two little girls dead in the bed. I can't roll over on this, I can't," Detective Boatwrite said. Captain Lawson took a deep breath.

"Boatwrite, we are talking about cop killers. Are you sure this is the road you want to take? I'm trying to protect you here and you as well, Detective Flowers."

"Respectfully sir, there is no protecting us. They already showed us they do not mind killing cops to protect us. We have to get them off the street because me and Detective Boatwrite know that Porscha Shields is behind all of this, and if we don't do something now, she will become the untouchable."

"Look… ninety days… you have ninety days to have some evidence on her to say who you say she is. Everything must be by the book. Do I make myself clear?"

"Yes, Captain, you do."

"Hey." Both detectives looked at him. "Y'all be safe out there." They both nodded as they walked out of his office.

***

Porscha was sitting in her office watching the news when Rakim walked in, smoking a blunt. Porscha looked at him.

"What you have to tell me, Rakim?"

"I found our golden boy's address where his daughter is getting married at."

"Good, what is the address?"

"It's 2114 Main Street, I even went to check it out myself and I'm glad I did. It's a park right next to the church."

"Oh, that's even better."

"Yeah, I thought that might put a smile on your face."

"When he is dead, that's when I'm really going to smile. Look, have someone pick up all the money from the projects and Club Mercedes. We have to get ready for this new drop, forty-five hundred kilos at twenty thousand a brick? That's nine million and we need to be able to cover that. He give us ninety days, but I want to pay him his money up front, it's better business that way."

"That's keeping him off your back as well."

"Yeah. After you get the pick-ups, have Corey come see me. I have a job for him."

"Cool, let me get on this now while it's still early." Porscha nodded as he walked out of her office to go handle the business.

Chapter 19

Chris Salini sat behind his desk in his office, sipping on some Ciróc on ice as he read over a case file. When Detective Boatwrite and Detective Flowers walked into his office, he took a sip of his drink as they walked up to his desk.

"Detectives, what can I do for you?" Detective Boatwrite looked around the office.

"Nice office, this must cost a pretty penny. What, a hundred thousand? Two hundred thousand?"

"Somewhere in that ballpark. You never told me what I can do for you."

"We are here about a client you represented."

"I represented a lot of clients, so I don't know who you are talking about."

"Alverez Sliver, do the name ring a bell?"

"Yeah, it does, matter of fact."

"Good, because we need to know who paid you to represent him."

"Detective, what is your name?"

"Boatwrite, Detective Boatwrite."

"Well, Detective Boatwrite, I am not at liberty to pass that information off to you. I can get disbarred, attorney-client privileges. Sorry, I can't help you. The door is behind you. I was just going over a case file so have a nice day, Detectives."

"You know that man may be the reason why a judge is missing, and a district attorney is dead, and a mother and two daughters were killed last night."

"When you first started you said maybe, so maybe you should find out, Detectives. Now, again, have a nice day." Detective Boatwrite smiled and pointed her finger at Chris Salini before walking out of the office.

***

"Mannino, baby, I love you so much. But please, listen to me, our daughter's wedding we should push it back. Something don't feel right. This nigga bitch, she not scared, she not backing down, and the other families are acting like they don't care about this war," Mannino's wife Brooke said.

"I'm not doing that to my daughter. It's been a few days. Things have quieted down a lot so I'm just going to be on the lookout for all crazy movements. And I talked to the other families already. I told them I got this, so I just need you to trust me, beautiful, everything is going to be alright. I promise you that."

"Ok, I trust you, Mannino." Broke kissed Mannino's cheek and went upstairs. Mannino walked to the door and looked outside at his guards, watching the house in the SUV parked out front, before going upstairs with his wife.

***

"So, the attorney was a bust, so we back at point A. Where do we go from here?" Detective Flowers asked.

"I don't know, you know what? We need to look into Porscha a little more, check her background."

"I already did that twice, Boatwrite. She's clean, there's nothing on her, not even a jaywalking ticket."

"That just don't sound right. You think our friend, Agent Sampaio, could look into it for us?"

"Remember, he was suspended for working on this case? He might still be suspended for all I know."

Before Detective Boatwrite could say anything, there was a call over the radio. "Dispatch, we have a one-eighty-seven on Bayview Avenue, female." Detective Flowers answered the call

"Dispatch, this is Detective Flowers, I'm en route now to Bayview Avenue."

"Detective Flowers, ten-four."

"Come on, Boatwrite, let's see what's going on, on Bayview Avenue." It took them twenty minutes to get there. When they arrived, there were already three police cars out there. They stepped out the car and walked to the officer.

"Hey what we have here, Officer?" Detective Flowers asked.

"One Jane Doe, from the look of it she got her neck broken. The lady over there found her body in the dumpster when she was taking the trash out."

"Ok, Officer, thank you." Detective Flowers looked at Boatwrite.

"What you think?"

"Let's go have a look at the body first."

"After you." Both detectives walked to the dumpster and looked inside at the body wrapped up in plastic wrap from the shoulders down.

"She was just a kid, no more than twenty-five years old. Let's go talk with the lady who found her," Detective Boatwrite said.

"Come on." They both walked to the lady as she was standing there smoking a cigarette.

"Hey, I'm Detective Flowers and this is Detective Boatwrite. We need to ask you some questions."

"Ok."

"First, what is your name?"

"Melanie Young."

"Ok, Miss Young, what time did you discover the body?"

"About forty-five minutes ago. I was taking the trash to the dumpster and when I opened the lid, I seen her in there."

"And you work right here at Stouffer's Diner?"

"Yes, for the last year."

"Ok, wait here for a few seconds."

"Ok." Detective Boatwrite walked off with Detective Flowers

"I don't know what to think about this."

"Look, let's just get her to write a statement, and we will follow up on this in the morning."

"That sounds like a plan to me."

Chapter 20

Jimmy walked into the bar with a few other guys. He went up to Lucchese who was at the back table having a drink, smoking a cigar and watching the baseball game.

"Lucchese, I see you are still putting your money on them Mets, when are you going to learn?"

"Jimmy, you came way down here to talk shit about my Mets, or do you have something to say?" Lucchese said as he smoked his cigar laughing.

"You know I came down here to talk with you. I was in the Bronx making pick-ups and I saw that Porscha girl with a few of her bodyguards down there."

"Yeah, I had a talk with her already, we have an understanding."

"And what type of understanding do y'all have?"

"What can I say, Jimmy? I gave her an offer she couldn't refuse." Jimmy nodded.

"You would think Mannino would learn by now, three wars in two years, does this man have a death wish?"

"Sometimes a man don't get it until he is looking down the barrel of the gun and you know what? I like Porscha, she is a tough cookie."

"Yeah, I can tell. Are you going to Mannino's daughter's wedding?"

"Yeah, I'm going to go show my face out of respect. You should go too."

"Yeah, I'm going to stop by with a gift. But I have to get going, Lucchese. I'll see you at the wedding."

"Yeah, I'll see you there." Lucchese puffed a few more times on his cigar as he watched the game

***

Porscha was walking around her winery when she saw her attorney, Chris Salnini, walking in the door. She looked over at him and walked up to him.

"Now, this is new, you coming down here. So, did you come for the wine tasting?"

"As much as I love a good wine, there is no drinking for me today. I've come to let you know that two detectives, the same ones that pulled you over, came to my office yesterday. They're trying to find out information on Alverez Sliver, or who we know him by, Emilio Sanchez."

"I am getting real tired of these detectives all in my shit. You know what? Maybe it's time that I get back in they shit. I'ma need something from you, Salini."

"Sure, anything. What can I do for you?"

"All the information you can get me on both of these detectives… names, addresses, schools or daycares, family members' names. I'ma need it all."

"I can do that for you, just give me two days at the most and I will bring it to you personally."

"Thank you, Salini. Now come walk with me, I have something for you." Porscha walked Salini to the back of the winery where the VIP members were. She walked up to the higher bar and passed him two bottles, one bottle of Château Margaux 1996 priced at almost eleven thousand dollars, and another bottle of Chateau Lafite Rothchild 2009 priced at close to seventy-eight hundred dollars. These are on me to you, Salini, they are some of my best wines."

"Thank you, Porscha, I will enjoy drinking them. I'll have that information for you within forty-eight hours."

"Ok, thank you." Porscha watched as Salini left. She was shaking her head at all the weight that was on her shoulders. She smiled and walked up to some of her VIP guests.

***

Detective Boatwrite and Detective Flower's car pulled up at FBI Agent Sampaio's house in Brooklyn. They both got out of the car and looked around the neighborhood before walking up to his front door, knocking. After a few seconds, Sampaio came to the door and looked at both of them. He smiled as he opened the door to let them in.

"So what brings y'all way over here from Manhattan to Brooklyn?"

"Honestly, to see if you can help us," Detective Flower said.

"I don't know how much help I can be. They suspended me for seven months. I still have two more to go."

"I'm sorry they did that to you," Detective Boatwrite said.

"Yeah, but there's nothing we can do about it now. So, what can I help y'all with?"

"We can't find nothing on Porscha Shields, nothing at all, it's like she is a ghost."

"That's because she is protected. Before Stallone was killed, we were also looking into her. Her files are restricted, someone up the food chain is protecting her, Boatwrite."

"It's too much killing and it's like everyone is brushing this under the rug. Judge Smith's whole family is dead… wife, daughters, sister, and he are still missing. FBI Agents Ross and Stallone, two police officers. Mafia capo and cartel boss Juanito Sanchez, and every time we turn around, there are bodies upon bodies in the streets. And last night, me and Boatwrite went to a one-eighty-seven, where there was a girl no older than twenty-five in a dumpster, wrapped up in plastic wrap."

"Y'all know what I think, I believe that Estabon Sanchez had his son, Emilio Sanchez, come to America to kill his brother Juanito Sanchez, because Agent Ross was about to find out what the cartel was dealing with and how they were getting their drugs in America. That's why Juanito was killed, and whoever got Emilio Sanchez out knew they only had forty-eight hours before his fingerprints came back, so they was on a time frame."

"So, they kidnap the Judge Smith's family, and District Attorney Croughton's family, then kidnap Judge Brad Smith and District Attorney Shawn Croughton to show them we have your family, then somehow they kidnapped FBI Agent Paul Ross, the only witness to Juanito Sanchez's murder who would testify in court against Emilio Sanchez for killing his uncle. They kill him in front of both Judge Smith and District Attorney Shawn Croughton to show them they don't mind killing a cop. They let them go for court. Emilio Sanchez is set free, they let their families go and both Judge Smith and District Attorney Croughton resigned and moved, all within two weeks," Detective Flowers said.

"That sounds about right, Flowers."

"So, the question is, where do we go from here, how can we prove all of this?" Detective Boatwrite said.

"You are not going to want to hear what I'm about to say, but it's the truth. They are too powerful, their money is too long, there is no stopping them. The only way to stop this is to get them dead to the wrong and hope your name don't come up on their list."

"Do you think we are still dealing with the cartel?"

"Boatwrite, that ghost y'all are chasing, if you have to ask me, Porscha Shields is the Cartel. And she is planting her flag in New York and not even the mafia can stop her." All of them looked at each other, not saying a word.

***

Paris walked around the club, looking at all the VIP areas. She then walked upstairs to where the girls were getting ready for the club doors to open. She walked into the room and said, "This is our house, ladies. We all been through hell, but we are still standing, let's get this money. Remember, we are all doing this for a reason. That's why we are all here. Porscha wants fifteen hundred, but I know y'all could do twenty-five hundred a night. That's a thousand dollars y'all will have saved up that you can use for a rainy day, remember that." Paris walked out of the room, knowing it wasn't just the girls' lives on the line, but hers as well.

Chapter 21

Detective Boatwrite sat at her desk, going over Ms. Young's police statement when a yellow 10x13 legal envelope was placed on her desk, as well as Detective Flowers' desk. They both looked at each other at the same time as they opened the yellow legal envelope. Boatwrite couldn't believe what she was seeing. It was pictures of her mother at home working in the yard, but the picture was through the scope of a gun with the bullseye right on her mother's head. There were also pictures of her sister at work, and her uncle and his daughter at the daycare, all taken through the scope of the gun. She looked at Detective Flowers and she knew he had the same type of pictures by his facial expression.

There was a note also in there that said, "Find something safe to do before I find something for you to do every week. You have a lovely family. Next time it won't be a picture, it will be a head I send to you, starting with the baby girl." Detective Boatwrite's heart skipped a beat when she read that. She looked at Detective Flowers as he was reading the letter that was sent to him as well.

"Flowers. Flowers." Detective Flowers didn't say anything, he just looked at the picture of his daughter and son at school eating their lunch outside, with the scope of the gun pointed at them. Both his kids were only seven-year-old twins. He placed the picture down and read the note again. The note said, "History shows I don't mind killing. Alex And

Alexis will be the first to die. Find someone else to play with, because the next crime scene you get called to will be one of your loved ones. I'm not doing no more talking."

"Detective Boatwrite?"

"Yeah."

"I'm done, I'm off the case."

"Flowers, I got the same thing in the mail just now."

"I said I'm fucking done. I'm not talking about it no more." Detective Flowers got up and walked out of the office.

***

Detective Flowers was outside in the back of the police station, smoking a cigarette when Detective Boatwrite walked up to him.

"I told you already, I'm done, there is nothing to talk about."

"Flowers, trust me. I understand your fear, but we can't let her run us off like roaches when the light comes on."

"Do you hear yourself? They have pictures with our families, Boatwrite. I'm not going to bury one of my loved ones over this case I'm not I'm going to take a note out of District Attorney Croughton's play book and move my family and say fuck this case. Shit, we can't even find him. We looked everywhere. For all we know, he is dead too, and his family. And guess what, Boatwrite? This is not a risk I want to take. I'm done."

"We are so close, Flowers."

"You're right… to death. When are you going to see that?" Detective Flowers walked off and got into his car and drove off, leaving Detective Boatwrite standing in the back of the police station.

***

The black-on-black Cadillac Escalade platinum edition pulled up in front of Porscha's winery. It was 7:30 pm as Porscha walked outside and got into the Escalade. Once inside, the Escalade pulled off.

"Beautiful, how have you been?" Trayvon asked as he gave her a kiss on the forehead before pulling out his cigar and lighting it.

"I been good, Father. Just taking care of the cartel, that's all."

"By taking care of the cartel, what do you mean by that?"

"Making sure all money is counted for, and all projects we are working out of are running one hundred percent with no flaws."

"So, how do you plan on moving the next two shipments we have coming?"

"Through the mafia. We are still going to work out all of our projects in the Bronx, Brooklyn, Manhattan, and Club Mercedes. With what we have we are talking about twelve million a month, give or take, and with the mafia at thirty-five thousand a kilo, for everyone we sell, that's fifteen thousand we make on top of what we already have coming in."

"I like the way you are moving and thinking, Porscha. Within six months look how far we have come. Remember, the sky's the limit, there is no stopping us. There's something else I want you to know. There are two types of respects." Porscha paid attention to her father as he talked.

"The first respect is, respect of who you are as a person and businesswoman. The second respect is the respect that comes with fear, the fear that they know they can come up missing. Do you understand me?"

"Yes, Father, I do."

"Good."

"Also, Father, I want to pay Estabon Sanchez up front for the shipments we have coming. It's only nine million dollars and we have that already." Trayvon nodded his head.

"That don't sound like a bad idea at all, I'll look into that. And how is our profits coming along?"

"We have twenty-four million, ten million in the bank. I ran the money through Club Mercedes and the winery as well as a restaurant that I opened four months ago."

"Wait, two things. You opened a restaurant? And how was you able to put so much money into the bank?"

"Yes, Father. The restaurant is called Horizon Legacy. It's a private five-star restaurant in the lower part of Manhattan. I have a private party running the restaurant for me because it's a very high-end place. I paid the manager at the bank half a million to make sure everything is on the up and up, so no red flags. And the other fourteen million is in a safe, in the winery hiding a pass code. Your date of birth." Trayvon couldn't do nothing but smile when he heard that

"I see you have everything under control, but this is what I do want you to do. Keep the money in the bank, have Corey or Rakim bring me the other ten million. You keep the four million in the safe, and from here on out, in the end when we split up our profits after we get Estabon his money, have one of the two bring me my share."

"Ok, Father. I can do that."

"I love you, baby girl."

"I love you more, Father." The Escalade pulled back up in front of the winery. Porscha kissed her father on the cheek before stepping out the Escalade, going back into the winery. Porscha and Trayvon lived the same life, but on two different time frames. She controlled the night, and he controlled the day, and that's how they made it work.

***

Mannino sat on his couch with his rosary beads in his hands as he prayed. It was the first time that he prayed in a while. His wife came to the stairs and looked down in the living room at him praying. She walked downstairs and sat next to him on the couch and placed her hand on his shoulder. After he was done praying, he held the rosary beads in his hands as he looked at his wife.

"I didn't know you was up still."

"I was waiting on you to come home."

"I was just getting everything ready for tomorrow, that's all. It's our little girl's wedding and I want everything to be perfect for her."

"It will be, as long as we are there, that's all that matters."

"You are right about that, beautiful. Come on, let's go to bed, we have a big day tomorrow."

"I love you so much, Mannino."

"I love you so much more, Brooke."

Chapter 22

There were three hundred plus people outside in the park. The wedding theme was black and pink. Black and pink ribbons were all over the park, tied to the chairs along the tree branches. Two ice sculptures were visible, one was an elephant, and the other of a bald eagle. The parking lot was filled with cars. A Ferrari 360 Modena stretched limousine stood out amongst the other limousines. Sixty waiters catered to all the guests walking around in pink and black. There were gifts from everyone, over three hundred of them. Mannino's daughter Victoria was in a white and pink Louis Vuitton wedding dress. Her husband George was in a black and pink Louis Vuitton suit. They were taking pictures together by the ice sculptures.

"Mannino, your daughter had a beautiful wedding. I loved it, she is a beautiful angel."

"Thank you, Lucchese. It means a lot to me that you and the other families was able to come here today on my daughter's wedding day."

"Mannino, we wouldn't have missed this for the world. Now, it's getting late, I'm going to go get me a drink and head back to The Bronx."

"Take care, Lucchese, I'll catch you later."

Mannino walked over to his daughter and wife and took pictures with them. After taking the pictures, everyone walked up to his daughter and her husband to give them congrats on the outstanding wedding, it was four hours long.

People started to leave. Besides the family of the bride and the waiters and the guards that Mannino had there walking around, everyone went to take one last family picture together. Nobody noticed the four waiters that pushed their carts together as the family was taking the pictures.

That's when one of the waiters nodded at all of them. They pulled out the FM P90s with the switch on them and all everyone heard was gunshots going off in the park as they stood side by side, shooting everyone who was taking the family picture. Blood sprayed out of everyone's bodies as the bullets were ripping through them. One of the shooters turned around, shooting at the guards as they took cover.

Lance ran up to Mannino as he was on the ground, coughing up blood. Lance aimed the Np 90 at Mannino's face and said, "Porscha told me to tell your pussy ass before you die, her shooter don't miss." He then emptied the clip into Mannino's chest. One of the other shooters shot everyone in the head that was right there on the ground, and bullets were still flying everywhere. All four of them were shooting their way out the park. They jumped into the SUV they had parked out in the parking lot and peeled off.

One of the guards ran up to Mannino and just looked down at his dead body, along with the rest of his family. It was thirteen in all that was killed. Within twenty minutes, the park was flooded with police, over forty of them. They had everything taped off with three local news teams shooting live.

***

Porscha sat in her office, drinking some Gray Goose on ice as she watched the news. She looked at the box of Cuban cigars and opened the box, and for the first time she lit one and said out loud, "I am that Boss Bitch." She then continued to watch the news, knowing her shooters didn't miss. This was more than a hit, this was a message she sent to everyone that she is not to be played with.

***

"I can't believe this shit. Who the fuck would do this? There are sixteen dead people, thirteen over there and three over there, Mannino Caporegime dead, another mafia boss." Captain Lawson looked around at the scene as CSI was out there working, and three news teams live on the scene. Detective Boatwrite looked at Captain Lawson.

"Do you know what the news is calling this?"

"No, lay it on me."

"The Wedding Day Massacre. No, Sunday the 15th Wedding Day Massacre."

"So, Detective Boatwrite, are we in the eye of the storm, yet?"

"Sir, this is a whole new forecast, this is a tornado mixed with a volcano that just exploded in New York City."

"Detective, I don't know what you and Flowers do in these streets. But whatever y'all do, I need y'all to do it fast, because right now all I see is the war on crime bosses." both Captain Lawson and Detective Boatwrite looked around, still not believing what they were in the middle of.

***

Lucchese was watching the news at the bar when Big Pete walked in, along with Tony.

"Lucchese, I see you are watching the news. Do you hear what the fuck they are calling this? Sunday the 15th Wedding Day Massacre. That is Italian blood mixed in with dirt, because of this nigga bitch!" Lucchese puffed on his cigar and stood up.

"Come on, we can go to the back and talk in my office, Pete." Both men followed Lucchese to his office. Once the doors were closed, he looked at them.

"Mannino made his bed and this ain't the first time that a war started because of him. Millions of dollars were lost because of this war. Two weeks before this Sunday the 15th Wedding Day Massacre, we shared a cigar and talked, his mind was made up. So, this is the outcome now. The only question is, who is going to take over the family in Manhattan?"

"So, you are telling me, this bitch kills a made man and his whole family in cold blood on the day of his daughter's wedding, and we don't do nothing about it?"

"Here's the thing, Pete, let me be real clear for you. Porscha is not to be touched. This war is over. The next person that goes after Porscha will meet the same fate as Mannino and his family. Now, if you don't mind, I would like to go back in the bar and finish watching the news." Lucchese opened his office door so they could step out and leave his bar.

***

Detective Flowers walked into the captain's office with the yellow 10x13 legal envelope in his hand, Captain Lawson looked at him.

"What do you have there, Flowers?"

"The reason I'm asking to be taken off this case, Captain."

"Wait, you want to be taken off this case I thought this was what you and Detective Boatwrite wanted." Detective Flowers passed the yellow envelope to the captain and watched his facial expression as he looked at the pictures and was reading the note.

"Wait, this came here in the mail to you?"

"Yes, Captain, four days ago. Detective Boatwrite got one as well."

"So why am I just now hearing about this?" Before Detective Flowers could say a word, Captain Lawson picked up the phone and called Detective Boatwrite to his office. Within two minutes she was walking through his office doors.

"Yes, Captain, you wanted to see me?" After she said that, she looked at Detective Flowers sitting there.

"Damn right. I want to see you have a seat and close my door." Detective Boatwrite closed the door and took her seat in front of the captain's desk.

"Why am I just now hearing about this threat that's on both of y'all families?"

"Sir, with all due respect, detectives get threatened all the time."

"Since I'm just now hearing about this, both of y'all are off this case. Matter of fact, for the next sixty days, y'all are on desk duty."

"Captain, you can't do this!"

"I just did, now both of y'all can go." Detective Flowers didn't say another word, he got up and walked out of the office with Detective Boatwrite right behind him. Once at their desks, she looked right at him.

"If you ain't want to be on this case no more, that's one thing, but to get me taken off of it that's fucked up."

"Do you hear yourself? People are being killed behind this case. Look at what just happened. Sunday the 15th Wedding Day Massacre? These people are not playing, Boatwrite."

"You know, if you ain't got the guts for this job, maybe you should walk back into the captain's office and place your gun and badge on his desk." After saying that, she got up and walked off in a state of rage.

Chapter 23

Porscha's phone went off. She looked and saw it was Lucchese calling her, she smiled as she picked the phone up.

"Hello, Lucchese."

"Good morning, Porscha. I was calling to see if we can have a meeting today?"

"Sure, how about we meet today around 2:00 pm at Horizon Legacy. It's a private restaurant in downtown Manhattan."

"Sure, that's perfect. Make sure it's a table of six, I have some people that would like to meet you."

"I'll make the arrangements."

"I'll see you then, Porscha."

"Likewise." Porscha hung up the phone and called to make the arrangements for the 2:00 pm meeting.

***

"We are not about to lay down, I don't give a fuck what that pink belly ass Lucchese says! Mannino was our don, Roberto was our capo, and they will not die alone, do you hear me?" Big Pete said as he looked at Tony.

"I hear you, Pete, and I stand with you on that."

"Good! You are my underboss. Joey is the capo. Get everyone together and let it be known family business is family business. If anyone speaks about our family business, they are going swimming with the sharks."

"I'll let them know, Pete." Pete watched as Tony walked off, knowing the line that they were about to cross, but he had to let it be known that he stood on business. He sat on the edge of the pool table, in deep thought about his next move.

***

The Mercedes Benz-Brabus G550 pulled up to a private restaurant called Horizon Legacy. Porscha stepped out looking like a runway model. She had on a Prada dress displaying her hourglass figure with six-inch open-toe red bottom shoes. Her hair was laid down. She had a pair of Prada glasses covering her face as she walked into the restaurant, headed to the back room where Lucchese was at with the rest of the families' bosses. Porscha had two Italian chefs that cost two thousand a week apiece, that were the main cooks at the restaurant. She'd made a call to her private party and made sure that the three specials of the day were three different types of pasta. Lucchese got up from the table and gave Porscha a hug and kiss on the cheek when she walked up.

"Porscha, let me tell you, I been in Manhattan for years and never knew about this place."

"Yes, this is a private restaurant, not everyone can eat here, only us that lives in the shadows."

"I see. Let me introduce you to the families' bosses. To the right is Lil John, then you have Nick the Boss, Big Pete, and Sammy the Don. Everyone, this is Porscha." Everyone nodded at her as she sat at the table with them.

Before she could say anything, the Italian waiter walked up to the table. Everyone was shocked when they saw him. He placed two family-size pasta broccoli cheddar bakes on the table, along with a basket of focaccia Italian bread. A few seconds later, the same waiter came back with two buckets filled with two bottles of Dalmore thirty-five-year-old Single

Malt Scotch whisky and a bowl of peanuts. Nick the Boss picked up the bottle of Dalmore.

"Talk about the high shelf." The waiter placed plates down in front of everyone and put pasta on the plates.

"This pasta is to fucking die for, swear to God," Big Pete said as he was eating.

The waiter smiled and said, "Can I please take y'all orders now? The pasta and Italian bread were just the appetizers, until the main course is ready."

Lucchese said, "How about you bring all of us the specials of the day?"

"Sure, your orders will be ready in forty-five minutes." The waiter walked out after saying that.

"Ok, let's talk business," Lucchese said.

"Yes, let's talk business. So, gentlemen, I want to thank everyone at the table for meeting with me today. I am sure Lucchese has talked with all of y'all here already of what I could bring to the table."

"Yes, he told us, but how do we know you have what you say you have?" Nick the Boss said.

"You make a good point but let me say this. If I ain't have it, I wouldn't be sitting at this table with y'all right now, but I like for my word to mean something. So, let me show you." Porscha opened up her Prada bag and pulled out a kilo of cocaine and passed it to Nick the Boss.

"So, how much are we talking about per kilo?" Big Pete said.

"Thirty-five thousand and the price is the price. I will not lower it."

"How much can you supply?"

"As much as you need."

"And is your deliveries guaranteed?"

"I don't think nothing in this world is guaranteed, Nick, but there will be insurance on your money. That I can promise you. Now, let's talk about what y'all can do for me."

"You will be protected in all the five Boroughs as long as you keep your end of the deal and stay in Polo Grounds, Manhattan, Brownsville Houses, Brooklyn, Castle Hill Houses and Patterson Houses in The Bronx, and Club Mercedes."

"Y'all have my word at this table."

"Good, now let's all take a shot to that." Nick the Boss said. As they took their shots, the food came to their table.

***

Trayvon smiled when he saw Estabon, he walked up and gave him a hug.

"Trayvon, it's good to see you again."

"Likewise. I have something for you."

"And what do you have for me, Trayvon?" Trayvon smiled and got the two duffle bags of money and placed them down on the ground in front of Estabon and opened them up.

"Nine million dollars."

"Is it blood money?"

"That's the only type of money." They started laughing.

"Forty-five hundred kilos, let's get them to America."

"Estabon, New York City is only the start." Estabon smiled as he patted Trayvon on the back. Over the next four months, Estabon had shipped over eighteen thousand kilos to New York. Porscha had New York City in a headlock. Everybody was making money, there was no stopping them. Horizon Legacy was the restaurant they ate at once a month, her and the five mafia families. New York City had a wave of cocaine like they'd never seen before.

Chapter 24

"Big Pete, are you sure you want to do this?"

"I been ready since the day of the Sunday the 15th Wedding Day Massacre to kill Lucchese."

"Do you understand the blowback this is going to cause?"

"I'm not worried about the blowback, fuck the blowback. I just need the job done." Big Pete looked at Jimmy the Hitman as they walked around the junkyard in New Jersey as Big Pete's car followed close behind them.

"The price is sixty grand, if you want him dead, money up front. Once I get the payment, I'll give you the date and time he will die."

"How will you kill him?"

"How you want him to die? Car bomb, gunshot, how do you want his death to come? Crowbar to his head, real bloody, it's up to you."

"I want his death to be real bloody, in his house with his wife and kids. I want all of them dead."

"That's going to cost more. I'll do it all for two hundred grand."

"Done. I'll have the money to you within seventy-two hours."

"Call me when you are ready for the pick-up."

"I will." Big Pete turned around and walked back to the car and got inside and lit his cigar as he looked at Tony.

"Lucchese and his family will be dead within seven days."

"Are you sure? Because right now we are all having our way, and it's because of Lucchese and Porscha."

"Fuck Lucchese and fuck Porscha. After we kill Lucchese, Porscha's ass is next."

"Whatever you say, boss. I'm with you."

***

"Captain Lawson, please come in and have a seat. This is Mayor Rapkin and FBI Senior Chief Goldwyn. They are here upon your request." Chief Hamrick sat down in the briefing room as Captain Lawson talked.

"Thank y'all for coming. Let me get started so I don't waste y'all time. Over the last year it's been a war on crime bosses, and a war on law enforcement. At the top of the food chain, it was cartel boss Juanito Sanchez. Then you had Roberto Reddinger, mafia capo. Next was Tyler Costen mafia councilor, then mafia don Mannino Caporegime. All crime bosses are dead. Now we have FBI Agent Paul Ross and FBI Agent Derrick Stallone, District Attorney Sandi Smith, Judge Brad Smith's family. And Judge Brad Smith is still missing.

"Every one of these law enforcers are dead and by now, we can only think the worse for Judge Smith. Now the name that keeps popping up is Porscha Shields. Since she hit the scene, crack cocaine flooded the streets of New York City. All five Boroughs are flooded with crack cocaine, and I am one hundred percent sure she is the one that's pushing the button on dropping bodies."

"Captain Lawson, if I may?"

"Sure, Mayor Rapkin."

"I been in New York City my whole life and I have never heard of a female over the mafia, and not just a female, but a black one."

"Captain Lawson, Mayor Rapkin is right. A black female killing mafia bosses and law enforcement officers? I think you are pushing it just a little here."

"Respectfully, Senior Chief Goldwyn, Porscha is not just Black. Her mother is Spanish."

"Ok, her father is Black, and her mother is Spanish. Why you think she may be doing all the killing then?"

"Name one king or queen who ain't drop a few bodies on the way to the throne, Mayor Rapkin. Let me tell you, Porscha Shields is becoming too powerful. Soon, she will be the untouchable."

"The FBI was looking into this case, but after FBI Agent Paul Ross was found dead, we searched his house and found drug, money, and text messages in his phone where he tipped the bad guys off. Paul Ross was a dirty agent, so the whole case was thrown out. Now we all hear what you are saying, Captain. Now let's say this. This Porscha Shields person is running New York City? What proof do you have? Because right now all I hear is someone chasing witches and I don't have time to go on a witch hunt, Captain."

"I don't have no proof of all this, that's why I need the funding to put a team together so I can prove it. This is about one name, one person, Porscha Shields."

"No. I'm sorry. Chief Hamrick, Captain Lawson, enjoy the rest of y'all day," Mayor Rapkin said as he got up and shook their hands as he walked out the briefing room with FBI Senior Chief Goldwyn.

"Captain, we tried."

"Yeah, that's the thing… only we tried," Captain Lawson said as he walked off

***

"Paris, we have a problem downstairs on the floor," one of the girls told Paris.

"What's going on?"

117

"One of the guys took the money back from Faith, she fighting with him now." Paris rushed out her office downstairs to the main floor, where her guards already had the guy on the floor, dragging him to the back of the club and out to the garage. Paris walked into the garage, gun in her hand as the bodyguards held the guy up against the wall.

"So, you come up in my spot and put your hands on one of my fucking girls, then try and take the money back she just earned from your ass?" Paris grilled him hard.

"Six hundred dollars for five minutes, that's a rip off." Paris looked at Faith.

"Six hundred dollars for five minutes, Faith?"

"I told him the VIP is two hundred and all events that go on back there are four hundred dollars. So, if I'm sucking your dick and you nut, that's four hundred dollars. It's not my fault he came in three minutes."

"If she told you that then that's what it is, but here's the big problem. Look at her face, look at what you did to her. Now that's something that I can't turn the other cheek on."

"Fuck you and fuck this club."

"I'm not doing no more talking, beat him down now." Paris watched as they punched him in the face and punched him in the ribs. He fell to the ground, and they kicked him all in the face until he was laying on the curb not moving, balled up.

"That was for you putting your hands on Faith. Now this is because I don't trust you and there is a chance you will go to the police, and I don't need that type of heat on this club." Paris pointed the gun at his head and pulled the trigger, painting the floor with his blood and brains.

"Y'all clean this mess up and make sure you drop his body off on the other side of town. Faith, you get back to work."

"Yes, ma'am." Paris walked from the back, headed back to the main floor to her office. That was her second time killing someone in the club, but she knew it wasn't going to be her last.

***

"Porscha, what's that look on your face mean?" Rakim asked her.

"I just got a phone call that Captain Lawson is trying to put a team together to come after me. He had a meeting with the mayor and chief of the FBI yesterday."

"So, you want me to go roll his ass?"

"No, it's been enough police killings. I just want to shake him up a little bit, that's all."

"What you have in mind?"

"Have someone put a bomb into his car and blow it up. Do it at his house, so he will get the picture it could have been his house."

"Say less, I'm about to do that now."

"Good, let me know when it is done."

"Will do." Rakim walked out of the office as Porscha sat in her chair, watching the news and lighting her cigar up.

Chapter 25

Captain Lawson sat in his office, drinking a cup of coffee with rum in it as he smoked a Newport, waiting on Detective Boatwrite and Detective Flowers to come into his office. That's when he heard the knock at his door.

"Come in." When the door opened up, Detective Flowers and Detective Boatwrite walked into his office.

"Come in and have a seat."

"What's going on, Captain?" Detective Boatwrite asked.

"I had an hour-long meeting with the Mayor and FBI Senior Chief yesterday about Porscha Shields. They are not trying to touch this case at all. On top of that, they are saying FBI Agent Paul Ross was dirty. They found some drugs and money in his house, with some other things."

"Captain, you know this is some bullshit, we all do."

"Boatwrite, I been down with you on this case from the start. We need to face the fact that Porscha is too strong. Too beat her we need to find out who is protecting her, that's the only way."

"So, what are you saying, Flowers, you want back in?"

"Yeah, let's get this bitch the old-school way."

"Captain, we both know the risk at hand. Let us bring her down."

"Whatever you do, just know there is no rewinding the hands of time, so whatever blood is spilled, it's on your hands."

"We got this, Captain," Detective Boatwrite said as they got up and walked out his office.

***

The black Town Car pulled up in the back of the lumber yard. Tony opened the door and stepped out, with a yellow envelope in his hand as he walked up to Jimmy the Hitman who was standing there smoking a cigarette.

"This came from Big Pete, two hundred thousand large, in big bills just like you asked. And here is the address where you can find Lucchese at." Jimmy the Hitman opened the large envelope up and looked inside, then closed it back.

"Let him know he will be dead in seventy-two hours." Jimmy the Hitman threw the cigarette down on the ground and turned around and walked off. Tony looked at him then he got back into the black Town Car and drove off, knowing the hell that's about to break loose when Lucchese is dead.

***

Captain Lawson sat in his house, on the couch in the living room. He cut the TV on and put it on the news. He shook his head as they were still talking about the war on crime bosses and the Sunday the 15th Wedding Day Massacre. The only thing he couldn't believe was that it was a female who was calling the shots, and she was not to be played with. She took New York City by storm. The only thing was, nobody in the streets was saying her name or talking about her.

That's what was making it hard to believe that she was who they said she was, because in his eyes, Porscha was a ghost. His thoughts were interrupted by a knock at his front door. He looked at his watch and saw it was 9:45 pm. He grabbed his gun from the end table and walked to his front door and said, "Who is it?"

Nobody said a word. He took a deep breath and swung his door open. He looked around but nobody was there. That's when his car exploded, blowing him back into his house on the floor. The explosion was so loud it broke out his house's windows in the front. He got up in a daze holding onto the door frame to keep himself up, as he looked at his car in full flames in his driveway. Within twenty-nine minutes he had the fire department and three police cars, along with Detective Boatwrite and Detective Flowers, at his house.

"Captain, are you ok?"

"No, I'm not, Boatwrite, that bomb could have went off in my house."

"She wasn't trying to kill you. She just wants you to feel her presence."

"Yeah, Flowers, but she brought this to my house so shit just got real."

Chapter 26

Lucchese walked to his car where his driver was waiting on him with the rest of his family. He was taking his wife and kids to an Italian restaurant in Manhattan to eat lunch. He had both of his bodyguards following behind him in another car. He got into the SUV, his driver closed the door and got into the car and drove off.

"So, Angel, how are you doing in school, young lady?"

"I'm doing good, Daddy. I'm passing all my grades."

"And what about you, little champ?"

"I'm passing all my grades too, Dad, because I want that bike you promised me."

"And when I see it on your report card… if you are passing them grades, you will get that bike, little champ."

"And what about me, Dad?"

"Angel, I know you want that little puppy, so if your grades are passing too, you are going to get that puppy you want. Now this restaurant we are about to eat at has, hands down, the best pasta I ever ate. It's going to knock your socks off."

***

"Porscha, Captain Lawson got the message last night loud and clear. I watched the whole show."

"Good, maybe now he will understand who he is dealing with, Rakim. So yesterday, I got a call from Paris. She told me that she had to send someone to their maker."

"For what?"

"She said he jumped on one of the girls and took his money back."

"So, she kills the man?"

"Yeah, but you know what, Rakim? It's good that she did that. It shows the girls that we always have their back and that we are there to protect them at all times."

"Yeah, it does. So, what she do with the body?"

"She had his body dumped off in Queens. She said make it look like a robbery."

"Now that was smart." Porscha nodded as she looked out the window as the SUV was pulling up to her winery.

"Come, Rakim, we have to count up Estabon's money for our next two shipments."

"That should already be done. I told Corey take care of it already."

"You know I like to double count everything."

"I already know," Rakim said as they stepped out of the SUV.

***

"Captain Lawson, from the 27th Police Station, his car blew up in his front yard last night," Judge Miller said as he looked at Mayor Rapkin as he placed the newspaper down

"Yeah, what a night he had. He should know his place in life now. Maybe he got the picture now."

"I hope so, Rapkin. I would hate to go to another cop's funeral."

"Let's hope that's not the case. I was very clear when I said don't kill him, just shake him up a little bit."

"I know you was. By the way, our friend dropped this off for you last night. I told him I would bring it to you this afternoon." Adam passed Rapkin the envelope. Rapkin opened it and looked inside.

"How much is in here?"

"Eighty thousand dollars."

"Damn, Adam, I like the way he do business."

"Me too, Rapkin," Adam said as they sat at the country club having drinks with each other.

***

Captain Lawson sat at his desk talking with the chief of the police station.

"Lawson, you are good police but let me tell you something. This goes way above my pay grade. You could have been killed last night. The senior chief of the FBI don't want to touch this case."

"She ain't want me dead, she just wanted me to know she knows about me. That was a message, that's all, Chief."

"It could have been a deadly one, remember that."

"Chief, it was only four of us in that meeting. Me, you, Mayor Rapkin and Senior Chief Goldwyn. Not even seventy-two hours after the meeting, my car blows up. Someone tipped her off."

"Look, let me see what I can do, I have a few friends I can call. Let me try and find some phone records and see what I can dig up."

"You sure you want to do that? Your head can be on the chopping block next if she finds out what you are doing."

"I got this. You just keep your head down, while I do what I have to do."

"Say less, Chief." The chief got up and walked out of the office, knowing the battle he was putting himself in. He closed Captain Lawson's door. He knew this was going to be a long fight.

***

Jimmy the Hitman sat in the parked van across the street. He had his hand on his gun as he watched Lucchese and his family leaving the restaurant. He'd been watching them since last night and he'd been following them all day. Lucchese walked out of the restaurant with his wife, holding her hand when Jimmy the Hitman pulled the trigger. The impact of the bullet blew Lucchese's wife back into the restaurant. Lucchese jumped in front of both his kids, using his body as a shield.

Jimmy the Hitman was shooting the restaurant up, Lucchese's bodyguards were shooting at Jimmy the Hitman, bullets were flying back and forth. Lucchese looked at his wife coughing up blood. One of Lucchese's bodyguards got shot in the head by Jimmy the Hitman. Lucchese ran out of the restaurant shooting his .38 snub nose at the van as he pulled off, hitting Jimmy the Hitman in the head, killing him and making him crash into a parked car. Lucchese's bodyguard ran to the van and opened the door and looked at Jimmy the Hitman's dead body fall out the van to the street. Lucchese ran across the street and looked at his dead body as well.

"Jimmy the fucking Hitman, son of a bitch!" Lucchese yelled out as he held his gun in his hand.

Chapter 27

Porscha sat down in her office, watching the news. She couldn't believe what she was seeing and hearing. Her eyes and ears were glued to the TV screen as the news reporter was talking. She didn't say anything when Rakim and Corey walked into her office and started watching the news.

"Today on Patterson Road, at Per Se five-star restaurant, mafia boss Lucchese Bonanno was eating out with his wife and two children, when an assassination attempt was made on his life. His wife, Brooke Bonanno was shot, with life threatening injuries. She is at the local hospital undergoing surgery. The shooter was killed, along with one of Lucchese Bonanno's bodyguards. The shooter was identified as Jimmy Hicks, also known as Jimmy the Hitman, who is also a hired gun for the mafia. Keep your channel turned in here for more updates as we run the story on mafia boss Lucchese Bonanno, and the story on Sunday the 15th Wedding Day Massacre as the war on mafia bosses go on in New York City." Porscha placed her hand on her head as she looked at Rakim and Corey before talking.

"Shit just hit the fan, make sure y'all have extra guards around here and Club Mercedes. These pasta eating motherfuckers ain't going to do no talking right now. Everyone is a suspect."

"But they should know we ain't sending no Italian to kill no Italian. We have our own shooters for that."

"They are not going to give a fuck about that, Corey. Right now, all Lucchese wants is blood."

"I'm going to let everyone know to be on point, and beef up the security, just in case they do try something."

"Ok, Rakim. Corey, go downstairs and do a count and send all the workers home until I can figure the shit out."

"Ok, I'm about to do that now." Porscha knew shit was about to get ugly and there was no stopping the bomb that was about to blow a hole in New York City.

***

"My wife is in ICU. Someone tried to have me killed, my wife was almost killed, my fucking kids was shot at. I held my wife in my arms as she coughed up blood. Someone hired Jimmy the Hitman to kill me, and I want to know who. I want every rock dug up, until this motherfucker is brought to the light so I can personally skin his ass alive." Lucchese sat in the bar around his mafia family as they stood around looking at him as he talked in rage.

"Lucchese, what about Porscha. You think she had her hand in this?"

"I won't know until y'all find out, now will I, Tommy? So, everyone hit the streets now." All Lucchese could think of was killing the son of a bitch who tried to kill him and shot his wife. He was about to show New York what war really was.

***

Big Pete walked the floor at his house as he smoked a cigar talking to Tony.

"How the fuck did he miss his target?

'I don't know, but they say it was an all-out shootout before Jimmy was gunned down, Pete."

"I don't give a fuck about an all-out shootout at all. I paid for him to kill Lucchese and his family, not to get himself killed. Now look at this fucking mess. They are talking about this on the news, and I know Lucchese has his goons out there right now, looking for answers."

"Boss, don't nobody no nothing, nothing can come back to us at all. Only three people knew about the hit. Me, you, and Jimmy… and Jimmy is dead, so we are in the clear."

"No, you are wrong. Four people knew about the meeting, my driver Jo Jo. He brought me to the very first meeting at the junkyard."

"You think Jo Jo will run his mouth off?"

"I don't know, but I don't know if I want to take the chance to find out." Big Pete puffed on his cigar as he paced the floor.

"Let's give it two weeks to see how things play out, before we start dumping bodies in the East River."

"Tony, keep your ears open, and if you hear anything let me know, because a war is coming our way." Tony nodded his head before walking out the house. Big Pete puffed his cigar thinking about killing Jo Jo to tie up all loose ends.

***

"You know Flowers, something just don't feel right about all of this."

"What you mean? I need you to be more clear on what you are talking about, Boatwrite," Flower said looking at her at her desk.

"The captain's car gets blown up at his house, not even seventy-two hours after his meeting with the mayor and Senior Chief Goldwyn of the FBI. Then a few days later, mafia don Lucchese almost got killed. We been going about this all wrong. We need to follow Mayor Rapkin. He's the key to all of this, he's the one pulling the strings." Flowers looked at Boatwrite as he took a sip of his coffee.

"So, you want to go after the mayor, the head motherfucker in charge?"

"We need to follow the money. That's the only way we are going to get anywhere on this case."

"Fuck it, let's follow the money." Flowers got up and got his car keys and walked out the office with Boatwrite.

***

"Lucchese, we been talking to all of the families. Everyone sends their love to you and they best wishes to your wife on her recovery."

"Joey, I don't give a fuck about nobody sending me they love, or best wishes on my wife's recovery. I want the motherfucker who sent the shooter who tried to kill me and my fucking family," Lucchese said as he sat in the bar taking shot after shot.

"Ok, Boss, I'll go hit the streets again."

"Joey, when you come back, have something to tell me beside someone love and best fucking wishes."

"I'll do my best, Lucchese." Lucchese nodded then looked at Frankie.

"Did you go talk to Porscha to see if she knew anything?"

"No, Lucchese. Jimmy was Italian so all that tells me it was an Italian who put the hit out on you."

"Still, she might know something and if she knows something, then I need to know what she knows."

"I'll go talk to her first thing in the morning and see what she heard, Boss."

"Frankie, somebody knows something, and I'll bleed every fucking family out until I know what the fuck it is." Lucchese puffed on his cigar after saying that with anger in his voice as he watched as Frankie left.

Chapter 28

The black Cadillac Escalade pulled up in front of the winery. Porscha walked outside to the Escalade where Trayvon was waiting on her. The driver opened the door for her to get inside the back seat.

"How is my baby girl doing?"

"I'm doing good, Father, with all of this BS going on, it's just another Friday to me."

"Yeah, I saw the news and heard the story of what happened. Does Lucchese know who tried to kill him?"

"No, nobody is talking."

"Somebody is always talking, and somebody always knows something. You know what I want you to do? Kidnap Big Pete's driver and see what he knows. I'm willing to be my life on it that he knows something."

"Why him? Why Big Pete?"

"Because Big Pete may still have some pressure about Mannino being killed, and the only one who could have told him to stand down is Lucchese. If he kills Lucchese then he can go after you next."

"Now that you said it like that, that does make sense."

"Get the driver and you will get your answers. Now we are getting two shipments this week, so be ready to push them to the streets. And I'ma need eighteen million so have someone count that up. I'll be back in seventy-two hours for the pickup."

"Ok, Father, it will be ready." Porscha kissed Trayvon before getting out of the SUV.

***

Lucchese stepped out of the black SUV, smoking a cigar with three of his bodyguards. He looked around and walked into Big Pete's bar. He walked right to the back table where Big Pete and Tony were sitting. Big Pete and Tony got up out of respect to Lucchese. Both men shook his hand and gave him a kiss on the cheek, as he did the same thing to them.

"Lucchese, how is your wife doing? She is in my prayers."

"She is in better condition now. Brooke is a fighter. But for the last few days I've been trying to put two and two together to see who would send a shooter my way. Whose balls are that fucking big?"

"Lucchese, you bring everyone together, the mob is seeing more money now than we had in the last ten years."

"You made a good point, Pete. So, you are saying anybody could be my enemy at this point in time?"

"I'm saying who would most likely benefit off you being dead?"

"I don't know. Who you think would benefit the most, Pete?"

"Porscha. You and her made the deal, so with you out the way, she no longer has to honor the agreement you two agreed on. And she is free to supply whoever she wants to in New York City."

"But the shooter was Italian, that's the catch-22 here, Pete. That means an Italian hired the shooter, Pete."

"So, we need to find out who she working with then."

"Yeah, let's do that then. Can I trust you to find out for me, Pete?"

"Yeah, you can, Lucchese"

"I'm glad I can put my trust in you, Pete"

"Us Italians have to stick together." Lucchese nodded at him as he got his lighter out his pocket and re-lit his cigar before turning around and walking away. Tony looked at Big Pete.

"What you think about that, Big Pete?"

"He just gave us the loaf of bread to drop breadcrumbs right to Porscha's front door, Tony," Big Pete said with a smile on his face.

Chapter 29

Lance watched as Big Pete's driver Jo Jo was leaving the coffee shop. He pulled out his phone and called Rakim. Rakim answered right away.

"Yeah, what you got for me?"

"Jo Jo, he is coming your way. I'ma bring the van around the corner now, sliding door open."

"I'm on point." Rakim hung up the phone and pulled his gun out. As Jo Jo was headed to his car, Rakim saw the van coming up slowly. Rakim walked up to Jo Jo and pressed his gun to his side. Jo Jo just looked at him.

"We need to talk, get into the van."

"If I don't?"

"You die right here, right now." Jo Jo didn't say another word. He got into the van and sat on the floor with Rakim's ad the gun pointed at his head as Lance drove off.

***

Jo Jo sat in a chair, holding the coffee, still not saying a word in the warehouse. Rakim still had the gun pointed at him, as well as Lance. That's when Porscha came walking up to them, they all heard the sound of her heels hitting the floor as she walked.

"Hey, I see y'all have our guest. I hope y'all been nice to him."

"Yeah, we have been," Rakim said. Jo Jo was sitting there shaking as he held the coffee in his hands.

"Jo Jo, we need to talk. I don't want to hurt or kill you, but you know I don't have no limits to the shit that I do. So, I'm going to ask you some questions and I just want some truthful answers. That's all, do you understand me?"

"Yes, I do."

"Good." Porscha nodded at Terry. Terry walked up with a gallon of gas and a pair of bolt cutters and placed them on the table in front of Jo Jo. Jo Jo started sweating when he saw that.

"Don't worry about that, Jo Jo, that's only if you lie. Then things are going to get very bloody and painful. So, let me ask you. Did Pete order the hit on Lucchese and his family by Jimmy the Hitman?" Jo Jo looked at the can of gas and bolt cutters, then at Porscha.

"I don't know all the details of the conversation as they walked and talked. I was ordered to drive the car twenty feet back as they walked in front of the car."

"When did they have this meeting?"

"Two weeks ago."

"Where at?"

"The junkyard in New Jersey. Then there was another meeting at the lumberyard with just Tony and Jimmy the Hitman."

"Why was there another meeting without Big Pete?"

"It was Jimmy's payment to take care of the job."

"Last question, who runs these junkyards and lumberyards?"

"Fat Sally. He runs them."

"What family is he a part of? I know I said last question, but now I need more information."

"He's not a part of no family, he's just an Italian who runs the junkyard, that's all. Big Pete has him under protection."

"Ok, thank you. Now guess what? You get to take a ride with us to go see Fat Sally."

***

Detective Boatwrite and Detective Flowers both walked into the private country club, where they were stopped at the door by the country club security guards.

"Excuse me, this is a private club, members only. I'm going to have to ask you two to leave," one of the security guards said.

"I have my membership card right here, let me show you." Detective Flowers pulled out his police badge and showed the security guard his badge and gun. "Now that I showed you my membership card, I think you need to step out the way, before I bring all of you to another private club that's not as nice as this one."

All the security guards stepped to the side as both detectives walked past them.

"Nice place, Boatwrite, wouldn't you say?"

"Yeah, all I see is the rich and powerful smoking thousand-dollar cigars and drinking seven-thousand-dollar bottles of wine."

"Do you see who I see all the way to the table to the left?" Detective Boatwrite looked and saw Mayor Rapkin, Judge Miller, and FBI Senior Chief Goldwyn sitting at the table, laughing with each other smoking and drinking.

"You have to be fucking kidding me. Come on, let's walk this way before they see us."

"I guess we followed the money to the pot of gold, so what now?"

"We leave now. We know why we wasn't granted the team Captain Lawson asked for, and I can put my life on the line that someone, if not all of them, know what happened to Judge Smith."

"I'll take that bet with you." Both of them turned around and walked out of the country club. As they were leaving, a black-on-black SUV pulled up and the driver stepped out and opened the back door. Trayvon stepped out of the SUV and fixed his tie before walking up the steps to the country club past Detective Boatwrite and Detective Flowers. Both of them looked at Trayvon as he looked directly into their eyes.

***

Lucchese was sitting down in the restaurant eating, when Poully walked up to him and said in his ear, "Lucchese, we been looking around and asking questions. Nobody knows nothing. At this point, we are just chasing ghosts."

Lucchese looked at him and grabbed the knife that was on the table and grabbed Poully's shirt. He pulled him to him and stabbed him five times in the stomach and chest and threw his body to the floor. He then picked up the chair and broke it over his back sas he yelled out loud, "Chasing ghosts? Chasing ghosts? Now you are a fucking ghost, so find out who fucking tried to kill me and shot my wife." Lucchese's bodyguards grabbed him and walked him out the back of the private restaurant, while the other guards picked Poully's body up and carried him out the back as well. Lucchese got into the SUV and lit his cigar and all he said to his driver was, "Take me to see my wife."

Chapter 30

The two big-body Cadillac Escalades pulled up in the junkyard and to the office doors. Terry stepped out of the Escalade and looked around before opening Porscha's door. Porscha looked at Jo Jo and said, "I'll be right back. Lance will keep you company while I'm gone." Porscha stepped out of the Escalade and walked inside with Terry and Rakim as Corey and three of her guards stood outside holding NP90s in their hands. Porscha looked at Fat Sally and then the two men that were in there with him. She took her glasses off before talking.

"Fat Sally, I don't know if you know who I am. Let me introduce myself, my name is Porscha and I was hoping you could help me out." Fat Sally looked at her then at both her guards and the ones outside standing guard.

"I don't know you, but I have heard of you. Porscha, what can I do for you?"

"I need to see your videotapes if you don't mind from two weeks ago." Fat Sally started laughing.

"I do mind. So, I can't help you, so now you can turn around and leave."

"It's always one, who always wants to do things the hard way. Fat Sally, are you sure this is the road you want to take?"

One of the guys said to Porscha, "You heard what he said, and I think it's best that you leave now, because you don't know who is backing us here." Porscha snapped her fingers and pointed at the guy. Rakim pulled his gun out and shot him dead in the head, killing him. He then pointed the gun at Fat Sally. Fat Sally couldn't believe what he'd just seen.

"Ok, let me try this again. Fat Sally, respectfully, I would like to see the surveillance tapes from two weeks ago please." Fat Sally looked at the dead man on the floor, then he pulled up the surveillance tape that he knew she was looking for. Porscha watched as Big Pete walked around the junkyard with Jimmy the Hitman.

"I see you knew what I was looking for. Now show me the one with Tony in your lumberyard." Fat Sally did as he was told, Porscha looked at Terry.

"Get both hard drives and come on so we can leave. Fat Sally, thank you. If I was you, I'd get ready for the storm that's about to come your way. You fucked up and let two people have a meeting on your property about the assassination attempt on Lucchese and his family. Just know you killed yourself." Porscha walked out of the office back to the trucks. She got in and looked at Jo Jo.

"Thank you, I'll drop you off where your car is at." Jo Jo knew he'd fucked up, but he'd get another chance to run because he knew he was a dead man walking.

***

Detective Boatwrite and Detective Flowers walked into Captain Lawson's office and closed the door behind them. Captain Lawson looked at both of them.

"This got to be good, I ain't have to tell you to close my office door. So lay it on me, what you got?"

"We followed the money and the three people we saw sitting around the pot of gold. Judge Miller, Mayor Rapkin, and Senior Chief Goldwyn, they are all working together," Detective Boatwrite said.

"Yeah, I know. Every avenue I tried to take was blocked, and there's no proof that she had my car blow up. So that road was a dead end for me. To go above they heads we need real proof, video recording, records, we need to be able to tie them in with the bad guy. Something to stick, because when we place them handcuffs on any of them, we are stepping in the line of fire."

"So, what you want us to do, Captain?" Flowers asked.

"Keep following the pot of gold, don't worry about nothing else. If we get them with the bad guys on tape, that's a close case they can't get out of."

"We are on it, Captain," Boatwrite said. Both detectives got up and walked out of the captain's office.

***

The white Tahoe pulled up in front of Porscha's winery. Porscha had three guards in front of her winery dressed in suits. Frankie and three of his men stepped out of the Tahoe and walked up the steps to the front doors. Frankie looked at all of her men and said, "I need to speak with Porscha. Let her know Frankie is here."

"No need, she already knows you are here. Follow me please."

All seven of the men walked inside the winery to the right to a private room where Porscha was at sipping on a glass of wine, looking out the back window.

"Excuse me, Porscha, Frankie is here to see you." Porscha turned around and looked at Frankie and his men as she walked their way. She walked up to Frankie and gave him a light hug.

"Hey, so tell me, what brings you by?"

"As you know already, Lucchese had an assassination attempt on his life, and we are still looking for answers." Porscha sipped her wine before talking.

"How is his wife Brooke doing?"

"She is doing good, really good, on her recovery."

"That's good, come let's talk in private over there, just the two of us."

"After you." Once at the table, Porscha poured him a glass of wine as she refilled her glass.

"Frankie, respectfully… I heard the stories, and I saw the news. Jimmy the Hitman was Italian so wouldn't Lucchese think maybe an Italian might have put the hit on him?"

"Trust me when I say we are looking at all avenues right now."

"What about Big Pete? How does Lucchese feel about him?"

"As I said, we are just looking for answers right now. He don't know who he can trust, so he feels the same about everyone right now."

"I can understand that. How do you feel about this situation we are all facing?"

"It's not my place to talk on it." Porscha nodded.

"I understand. I'm sorry I couldn't be a help, but can you please tell Lucchese that I need to speak with him ASAP?"

"I will." Frankie got up and hugged Porscha. He then finished his drink before walking off to his men.

Chapter 31

"Trayvon, look how beautiful the sea looks, it is so peaceful out here." Trayvon looked at the sea from the deck of Estabon's yacht as he smoked his cigar.

"It is beautiful out here on the water, Estabon."

"Do you know why I called you out here, Trayvon?"

"To go over details of the next shipment?"

"No, business is good, we already have a route that is working just fine for the both of us. I called you out here because you and your daughter's loyalty is respected here. So, tell me, how many bodies did you have to drop to take over New York City?" Estabon puffed on his cigar as he waited to hear what Trayvon had to say.

"New York City is a big city to take over, respectfully, we just made friends. My daughter lives her life in the night. Meanwhile, I live my life in the light. My daughter will never sit at the table with my friends, and I will never sit at the table with her friends. I don't know the body count, but what I do know is my daughter don't want the throne. She wants to be a ghost because what they can't see they can't stop."

"Your daughter is smart. What about you? You don't want to be the king?"

"Why be a king, when I'm a cartel boss in New York City?"

"I been watching the news. They say it's a war on crime bosses."

"Sometimes, murder is the only recipe for respect."

"And you know what, Trayvon? That's why you are a cartel boss because you understand murder is a part of the life we live. you can't have feelings in this life because feelings will get you killed" Trayvon nodded and puffed on his cigar after Estabon said that, taking in every word he said.

***

Frankie walked into the room and looked at Lucchese as he was sitting down taking shots of gin back-to-back.

"What did Porscha have to say?"

"Nothing, she asked about your wife's well-being, out other than that, she knew nothing. All she was saying was that it was an Italian shooter."

"Every fucking body knows it was an Italian shooter, tell me something I don't fucking know, Frankie." "Let me tell you something you need to hear. Nobody is going to talk, and we can't go to war with everybody. Let Big Pete do what he said he was going to do. While he is doing that, you get your mind right, because when it is time to go to war, we ain't doing no talking."

"You got that fucking right."

"And before I forget, Porscha wants to see you she said."

"I'm not talking to nobody until I find out who hired the hitman."

"Say less, Lucchese, you are the boss."

***

Big Pete picked up his phone and called Porscha. After the second ring, she picked up.

"Big Pete, to what do I owe the honor of this phone call?"

"Just a friendly conversation. Lucchese put me in charge of finding out who tried to kill him, and I'm looking at everyone in our circle."

"Y'all Italians are funny as fuck. I mean, just a funny ass sitcom that needs to be on ABC."

"You think the fucking mafia is a joke, little girl?"

"You better watch your mouth, Big Pete, before you end up like your friends. My shooters don't fucking miss."

"Is that a threat?"

"No, it's a promise."

"Good, because you just crossed the fucking line."

"See me in the streets, Big Pete. I'ma show you I don't do the chit chat." Porscha hung up the phone and called Rakim. He picked up on the first ring.

"What's the word, Porscha?"

"Big Pete, he's on the grocery list. I see these Italians only respect violence, so it's time for a body count. Let everybody know it's time to pop the bottle."

"Copy, I'm on that shit now."

***

Big Pete puffed on his cigar as he waited for Lucchese to pick up the phone. After a few rings, Lucchese picked up the phone.

"Big Pete, it's 10:30 pm. This better be good news," Lucchese said as he looked at his wife sleeping in bed.

"Porscha is the one who called the hit on you and your family."

"And how the fuck do you know this?"

"She just told me out of her own fucking mouth that us Italians are a fucking joke, and that we need to be on a fucking sitcom."

"The balls this bitch has. She's fucking dead."

"I'm going to take care of this one personally for you, Lucchese."

"Whatever you need, let me know."

"Will do." Lucchese looked at his wife one more time before walking out the hospital room.

Chapter 32

Lil John shook his head as he looked at Lucchese and Sammy the Don as they were all talking in the back of Lucchese's house.

"I just can't go for it. Why would she want you dead, of all people? And one thing I know about that tough son of a bitch, Jimmy the Hitman, he would never work for a nigga, no matter how much money is on the table. I just can't see it."

"Lucchese, Lil John has a good point. It's always been bad blood with Big Pete and Porscha. She done killed two made men in his family. This was just a good chance for him to try and take her down." Lucchese nodded as they talked.

"If Big Pete is using what happened to me and my family to go after Porscha, I will kill him my fucking self, do y'all hear me?"

"All I'm saying is that Porscha is bringing a lot to the table for all of us. She had no reason to want you dead," Lil John said.

"I'ma say this, Porscha's not going to back down. So, you need to make sure that what Big Pete is saying is one hundred percent true. Because once shots are fired, there may not be no coming back to the way things were."

"I hear you, Sammy the Don. Why don't you go talk with Porscha then, and see what you can get out of her?"

"For you I'll do that, Lucchese, before tomorrow evening."

"And if Big Pete is full of shit, I will personally kill him myself." Nobody said a word, they just all nodded at each other.

***

Detective Flower and Detective Boatwrite had been following Judge Miller all day. They followed him to the Sunset Hotel and watched as he went inside.

"Boatwrite, I may be wrong, but isn't Judge Miller married?"

"Yeah, he is, I'm sure of it."

"So why do you think he is here this late in the day?"

"There's only one reason I can think of, and it ain't to be with his wife."

"Should we go inside to see who the lucky girl is?"

"I thought you would never ask." Both detectives walked into the hotel and saw Judge Smith in the bar at a back table with a red-headed girl.

"Boatwrite, do you want to take some pictures of this?"

"I sure the fuck do, Flowers." They were at a table a few feet away, and Detective Boatwrite took her phone out and started taking pictures of Judge Miller with the girl at the back table. That's when Judge Miller got up with the girl and walked out the bar with her, his hand on her ass. Boatwrite took pictures of them from the bar until they were back in the hotel lobby.

"So, the honorable judge cheats on his wife, Boatwrite."

"Yeah, but this ain't shit, this just shows that he is a dog, that's all."

"But it's the start of our investigation on him. Hold on, I'll be right back." Detective Flowers got up and walked to the bar and got a plastic bag. He then walked to the table Judge Miller was at and with a napkin, he placed both glasses in the plastic bag, and then he walked back over to Detective Boatwrite.

"That was smart, let's go see who our young lady is now."

"Yeah, but before we go, let's go see what room they went into first."

***

Paris looked at the two Italian men walking around the club. Monica, one of her girls, walked up to them.

"Y'all looking to have a good time today?"

"Yeah, we are, sweetheart."

"So, what y'all think about coming to the VIP? It's three hundred to go back there, but I promise you will have a good time."

"Is that so?"

The black-on-black Cadillac Escalade pulled up to Club Mercedes. The driver opened the door for Porscha to step out with both of her bodyguards. All three of them walked into the club front doors, one of the Italians saw Porscha and nodded his head at her. Paris looked and she saw the whole play about to go down. The one Italian pushed Monica out the way as he pulled his gun out and started shooting at Porscha. People were screaming as bullets were flying.

Porscha's guards jumped in front of her and were shooting back at the Italians. Porscha pulled her gun out and was shooting at them, until one of the Italians grabbed Monica off the floor and was using her body as a shield. Monica got shot three times in the chest, one of Porscha's bodyguards got shot in the head. Paris came running down the stairs, shooting one of the Italians in the side, dropping him. People were ducking down.

"Joey, you need to get up or we are fucking dead."

"When I get up, we need to get to the door, I'm bleeding bad."

"I got you, come on." Joey stood up and ran to the door as they were shooting their way out the club. Once out the door, Porscha's guard started shooting at them in the parking lot as they were getting into the SUV and peeling off. Porscha looked at her guard as he walked back into the club, holding his gun in his hand. She looked around at all the people on the floor hiding behind the tables. There were three dead people, and other people who were shot. Big Pete just pulled up and pressed the button, now it was her turn.

Chapter 33

"So, let me get this right. You shot the club up and killed a few people. Joey gets shot but this bitch Porscha is still alive?"

"Big Pete, she had shooters everywhere. We was outnumbered and outgunned, we are lucky to have made it out of there alive."

Big Pete puffed on his cigar and nodded before talking.

"All that matters is the bitch got the message. She knows that we are coming."

"What you want me to do now, Boss?"

"Nothing, just be ready because I know she is coming back. And we will not end up in a pine box like everyone else."

"Ok, Boss." Big Pete knew a war was coming, but he was ready for whatever comes his way.

***

Frankie walked into the pool hall where Lucchese was smoking a cigar at the back table. Lucchese saw him and pointed at a chair for him to sat down.

"That look on your face tells me a story I don't want to hear, so what you got to tell me?"

"Big Pete's shooters missed last night, and a few people got killed in the crossfire."

"You know Porscha is two and oh. Big Pete needs to be ready. Did Lil John go talk to Porscha yet?"

"He's on his way now, I was told"

"One thing I know about Porscha is that she's not going to make a move on emotions. So, she's going to hear what Lil John has to say before she makes her move."

"I hope you are right, Boss."

"Get in touch with Big Pete and let him know we need to talk."

"I'll do that now, Lucchese." Lucchese just nodded as he got up and walked away.

***

The white SUV pulled up to Porscha's winery. Lil John and three of his men stepped out and started walking up the stairs to the winery. Four of Porscha's guards stopped them at the door as they held NP 90s in their hands. Lil John shook his head.

"I'm just here to talk to Porscha, that's all."

"And what makes you think she wants to talk to you?"

"I just want to stop things before it gets out of hand." Lil John looked past Porscha's guards as she started walking up to them.

"Porscha, I heard about Big Pete sending shooters your way last night. I'm just here to talk, nothing else."

"You can follow me to my office, just you."

"What about my men? I trust them with my life."

"That's the thing, Lil John. I don't trust them with mine. Bring one, nobody else." Porscha turned around and walked off. Lil John pointed at one of his guards and followed behind her.

Porscha sat down at the table in her office as she looked at Lil John.

"So, you came here to tell me something, or to tell me why you don't want me to strike back?"

"Look, words were said, and actions were taken. The report came back that said you said us Italians need to be on a sitcom that we are funny as fuck. Now, that's disrespectful."

"I did say that, and I stand on that. How would you feel if the same man that Lucchese has investigating his shooting, is the same man who sent the shooter at him and his family?"

"I feel that Big Pete needs to be skinned alive. What are you saying, Porscha?"

"Three of my workers are dead. I asked that Lucchese come talk to me personally out of respect, and instead I get bullets flying at my head."

"That's why I'm here now talking with you, Porscha."

"Lil John, let me tell you. When I am doing business with someone it's all about trust, honor and respect. I want to show you something after I show you this. All the deals that my cartel has with the mafia is off the table. Blood has spilled from y'all end. Rakim, if you would play the video, please." Lil John watched as the video was being played of Big Pete walking the junkyard with Jimmy the Hitman.

"That video you are watching is two weeks before the shooting at the restaurant." Lil John's face was bloodshot red.

"Play the next video, please." Lil John watched as Tony paid Jimmy the Hitman the money for the hits in the lumberyard.

"That son of a bitch, and he made all fingers point at you."

"Yeah, that's why I said what I said to him. See, I been known about this."

"If you been known, why ain't you come and let Lucchese know?"

"I told Frankie to let Lucchese know that I needed to talk with him ASAP."

"Why you ain't tell Frankie what you just told and showed me?"

"Would you believe me when I tell you I didn't trust Frankie?"

"How did you get these video tapes?" Porscha laughed.

"I kidnapped Big Pete's driver and made him an offer he couldn't refuse, and he told me everything. So did Fat Sally in New Jersey. So, let me say this for the record. All agreements are off the table now and Big Pete is a dead man walking."

"I'll let Lucchese know what I saw, and let's see who kills Big Pete and Tony first." Lil John stood up and walked off, along with his guard. Porscha just smiled as she lit her cigar.

Chapter 34

"Are you sure, Lil John?"

"I saw this with my own fucking eyes, both of them. and Tony paying him off."

"This rotten son of a bitch. Go get his driver and Fat Sally's ass now. I'm going to skin both they asses alive."

"And what about Porscha? This right here and her pulling away from the families is going to be a big blow on us, Lucchese."

"We will deal with that later. Right now, Big Pete is the only motherfucker I have in my eyes."

"I'll go get them, Lucchese." Lucchese puffed the cigar he had as Lil John walked off.

***

Big Pete hung up the phone and looked at Tony as he was walking into the office.

"You wanted to see me, Pete?"

"Yeah. I just got off the phone with Nick the Boss. He said that Lucchese knew it was me who sent the shooter at him. Jo Jo told Porscha. I knew I should have killed that son of a bitch when I had the chance."

"He's out front, do you want me to go get him?"

"Yeah, go bring his ass to the backyard."

"I'll have some guys with me, and I'll meet you back there." Tony walked off. Jo Jo was cleaning the car when Tony walked up on him.

"Hey, bring the car around back, Big Pete said."

"Alright, I'll be right back there." Jo Jo looked at the three guys walking to the back of the house. Big Pete never wanted his car at the back of the house. Jo Jo got into the car and looked at the guard at the front of the driveway and pressed the gas, peeling out of the yard. All three men ran to the street shooting at the car, shooting the back window out as Jo Jo was riding down the street. Big Pete ran to the front of the yard as they were shooting.

"Son of a bitch, stop shooting, we will get his ass. Come on, we need to pay Fat Sally a visit now, damn it."

Jo Jo was panicking and not paying attention when his car was hit from the side, crashing into a pole. Jo Jo hit his head on the steering wheel, knocking him out cold.

"Tony ain't that Jo Jo right there that just hit the pole?"

"That is that son of a bitch. Get over there and grab him before the police come." By the time Big Pete's car made it up the block, he saw the car was smashed into a pole, Jo Jo was gone, and people were standing around looking at the scene.

***

"Flowers, we got a name."

"On our girl from the hotel?"

"Yep, Jessica Long."

"Do we have an address?"

"It's 1020 Parkside Drive."

"Should we go pay her a visit?"

"I thought you would never ask."

"Good, I'm driving."

"So, here's the rap sheet on her. She's twenty-seven years old. Mother's name is Gwen, father's name is Derrick. She's never been to prison, but she did do a few overnights before in county."

"How do you think she got to know Judge Adam?"

"She's a beautiful female, Flowers, and he is a man with a dick."

"Well, let's see what she can tell us about Adam then."

"Good cop, bad cop?"

"No, let's both be the bad cops on this one."

"So be it." They both got into the car and drove off.

***

The black SUV pulled up to the junkyard. Big Pete and his men stepped out of the SUV and walked into the office building. There was a man standing behind the desk. Big Pete looked at him and walked up to him.

"Hey, where the fuck is Fat Sally at?" Big Pete asked.

"Shit, I don't know, he don't work here no more."

"What the fuck you mean he don't work here no more?"

"Like I said, he don't work here no more. He sold me the place last week for eighty thousand in cash and I ain't seen him since." Big Pete looked at Tony.

"This motherfucker. Come on, let's get the fuck out of here now."

"Big Pete, what about him?" Big Pete looked at him and pointed his finger at him.

"You want a job working for me?"

"I'm just trying to run a clean business. I'm not trying to get mixed up with no tough guys, respectfully."

"Ok, I respect that. Tony, kill him." Tony pulled his gun out and shot him three times in the chest and walked out the office building behind Big Pete.

"Big Pete, now what?"

"If Jo Jo told Porscha about this meeting, that means Lucchese knows about it now. Someone is going to come and talk to me about setting up a meeting, and that's going to be the one who tries to set me up. So, we just wait but send more shooters at Porscha. I want this bitch dead."

"Ok, I'll take care of it as soon as I get back, Boss." Big Pete nodded as he got into the SUV.

***

Lucchese walked into the meat factory, smoking his cigar, hearing a man being beaten. Lucchese looked at Jo Jo as his men held him up in the air by his arms, while the other one beat him with brass knuckles. His face was bleeding, and his ribs were broken. Lucchese walked right up to him.

"My wife was shot, and she almost died because of you and Tony, and that fat fuck, Big Pete. What, you ain't think I would find out?"

"I ain't have nothing to do with it. I swear to God. I was just the driver, nothing else, Lucchese. You have to believe me, man."

"I do believe you, but I don't give a fuck. Now you are going to feel my wife's pain." Lucchese took his coat off and placed it on the table. He then rolled the sleeves up to his shirt, pulled on his cigar, then placed it down in the ashtray and picked up a billy club.

"You know, Jo Jo, before you skin your kill, you have to beat it tender." Lucchese swung the billy club into Jo Jo's stomach as hard as he could. Jo Jo started coughing up blood.

"Boy, that felt good, let me do it again." Lucchese beat Jo Jo nonstop for ten minutes with the billy club. Lucchese's men let Jo Jo's arms go and he fell. Jo Jo was on the floor in his boxers, coughing up blood. Lucchese walked to the table and picked up his cigar and re-lit it. He took a few puffs and said, "Bring his ass to the meat hook. I'm not done with him yet" Lucchese watched as they dragged him to the meat hook. They looked at Lucchese. He nodded at them. Jo Jo was screaming as they hung his body on the meat hook. Blood was pouring out of his back on the floor.

"I told y'all when I found out who shot at my wife and kids, I was going to skin they ass alive. I wasn't playing. Like I said, you are going to feel my wife's fucking pain." Lucchese walked up to Jo Jo's body as it hung from the hook, with a sharp knife in his hand and the look of death in his eyes.

***

Detective Flowers pulled up to Jessica Long's house. Both he and Detective Boatwrite stepped out of the car and knocked on the door. After a few seconds, Jessica opened the door.

"Hey, can I help you, Detectives?"

"Jessica Long."

"Yes, that's me." Detective Flowers pulled out his handcuffs and pushed Jessica to the door and handcuffed her.

"Jessica Long, you are under arrest for prostitution. You have the right to remain silent. Anything you say can and will be used against you in a court of law." Jessica had tears in her eyes.

"Wait, wait, please. I can't go to jail," Jessica said. Flowers looked at Detective Boatwrite and winked.

"Who else is in the house with you?"

"Nobody, I swear." Detective Flowers walked into the house and sat her down in a chair. Detective Boatwrite placed a file down on the table.

"I'm going to ask you some real simple questions, I want some real simple answers. Do you understand me?" Detective Boatwrite said.

"Yes, yes."

"Good. What were you doing with Judge Adam Miller at the Sunset the other day?" Before she said anything, Detective Flowers opened up the file and showed her the pictures of her and Judge Miller from the other day at the hotel.

"He pays me to have sex with him every Thursday."

"How much does he pay you?" Jessica lowered her head

"Six hundred every time I meet them." Both Detective looked at each other when she said that.

"Who is them, Jessica?"

"It's so many of them, judges, district attorneys, lawyers."

"Where did you meet them at?"

"The country club."

"By whom, Jessica? Who introduced you to them?" Boatwrite asked.

"A guy named Kevin. I met him at a club. We talked and a few weeks later, he brought me to the country club."

"Look at these pictures, do you know any of these guys?" Detective Flowers showed her three pictures, one of Mayor Rapkin and one of FBI Senior Chief Goldwyn and the last one of Attorney Chris Salini. Jessica nodded her head at all of them.

"How do you know them?" Flowers asked.

"I slept with all of them more than five times."

"Do you want to buy your way out of prison, Jessica?"

"Yes." Flowers took the handcuffs off of her and looked in her eyes.

"The next time one of them calls you for a good time, you make sure you call me and let me know where you are going, and with who. Do you understand me?"

"Yes, I do." Flowers placed his card on the table and he and Detective Boatwrite walked out of the house.

"Damn, this is bigger than we knew, Flowers."

"Yeah, it's a lot of big wigs involved in this. Let's go tell the captain what we just found out."

"Yeah, let's do that."

Chapter 35

Frankie walked into the office at the junkyard and saw the dead body lying in a pool of blood. He looked around and walked back out of the office doors and got back into the SUV. As the driver pulled off, he pulled his phone out and called Lucchese. After a few rings, Lucchese picked up the phone

"Yeah, what do you have to tell me?"

"It's a mess in there. Blood is everywhere, and there's a dead body in there, but it's not Fat Sally."

"Big Pete is tying up loose ends."

"Yeah, that's what he is doing. So, what you want me to do now?"

"If you see anybody that's a part of his family, kill them. He wants a war, let's give him what he is asking for."

"I'll let the guys know now."

"I'll call you once I leave this meeting with Porscha and the other three families."

"Sure thing, Boss." Lucchese hung up the phone as his car pulled up at the private restaurant Horizon Legacy where he was having the meeting at. He stepped out of the car with his guards and walked into the restaurant to the meeting. When he got to the back Lil John, Nick the Boss, and Sammy the Don were already there. A few seconds later, they saw Porscha and her bodyguards walking to the back where they all were. She walked up and shook everyone's hand before taking her seat at the table, with her guards standing behind her.

"Porscha, we are all here to clear up the air, from this big misunderstanding," Nick the Boss said. Porscha just looked at everyone not saying a word. Sammy the Don looked at her.

"Porscha, this was all on Big Pete, that's what we want to clear up with you."

"Sammy the Don, this was bigger than Big Pete. No one at this table reached out to me to make a clear understanding this was on Big Pete, after my club was shot up and three of my people were killed. It was after the truth came out that y'all wanted to have this meeting. I personally told Frankie to let Lucchese know I needed to talk with him ASAP before things got to where they are now."

"Lucchese, is this true?"

"Yes, it is, Lil John."

"Porscha, we all work together as one, this was something out of our hands."

"I respect the mafia, I really do, but as I sat here and hear y'all talking I asked myself, does the mafia respect the Medellin Cartel? What y'all don't understand is that blood was spilled, and none of y'all came to talk to me before the button was pushed. So, here's the thing. The protection I was promised, I don't need it no more. This last event showed me it's useless to me. All agreed deals are off the table, and I will personally have Big Pete killed and anyone who is standing with him."

"Porscha, are you sure this is the road you want to take?"

"Lucchese, my shooters don't miss and just for the record, we are already on that road."

"Wait, the both of you, before we add on gas to this fire," Lil John said.

"Porscha, I see it in your eyes. You are ready to die on what you stand on. Let's talk new business, because you are right. We should have moved differently with you, before bullets were shot."

"New business. Lil John, six-thousand-dollar on the original price for one year, and Manhattan is now my Borough on good faith from y'all at this table." Lil John looked at everyone at the table. Nobody said a word, they all just nodded.

"Porscha, we need to talk."

"Respectfully, Lucchese, we have nothing to talk about no more. You okayed it for my blood to be spilled. From here on out, I will do all my talking through Lil John. Now, if you will excuse me, I have things I need to take care of." Porscha got up and walked out of the restaurant with her guards behind her.

"Lucchese, the man you had looking for the shooter, was the man who sent the shooter at you. Now look at the stronghold you put us in."

"We don't need that bitch. There are other plugs we can go through for our cocaine, Sammy the Don."

"Let's not fool ourselves. Porscha has the best cocaine we've seen in the last ten years. Just know, all this is on you."

"And I'm going to take care of it."

"Good, because right now Porscha has blood in her eyes, and she's going to make sure Big Pete is dead."

"No, she's not. I got them. That's my word." Sammy the Don looked at Lucchese and nodded.

***

Big Pete sat in his living room drinking a cup of coffee and smoking a cigar. He had armed men walking around his house. He looked at Tony as he walked into the house.

"What you got to tell me?"

"The families just had a meeting, and they all agreed to give Porscha Manhattan. I was just told."

"Fuck what they think. Manhattan is my Borough and it's going to stay that way too. I'm fucking dead, do you hear me?"

"I hear you, Pete, you know that I'm with you no matter what."

Before Pete could say anything, they heard a big crushing noise then gunshots. Big Pete dropped his coffee and cigar and ran and picked up his gun off the desk. Tony was at the window shooting his gun. Pete yelled to Tony, "Who the fuck is out there?"

"It looks like Lucchese and Frankie, Pete." Lucchese was shooting two Glock 40s at Pete's men. Frankie had an M16 in his hands. Bullets were flying everywhere. Lucchese had fifteen men shooting up Pete house.

"You fat fuck, you are dead. Do you fucking hear me, you are fucking dead!" Lucchese yelled out. Big Pete was in the window shooting at Lucchese's men. Tony opened the door and got shot in the chest with an M16. Big Pete watched as his body hit the ground.

"I'ma fucking kill you, Lucchese, you fucking nigga wetback lover."

Big Pete shot two of Lucchese's men, bullets were flying through Big Pete's house. Big Pete took off running to the back of his house. He looked around at all his dead men, he opened up the back door and ran out the house Frankie saw him and shot him in the back with the M16. Big Pete fell on his side, dropping his gun. Lucchese ran up to him and shot him four more times, while he was on the ground, he then spit in his face.

"Lucchese, we have to get out of here now, he's dead."

"Frankie, set the house on fire, then we can go." Within two minutes, flames showed in the house as Lucchese and his men got back into the SUVs and pulled off.

***

Detective Boatwrite and Detective Flowers walked into Big Pete's yard. The fire department, CSI, and about thirty officers on the scene.

"Damn, this looks like a fucking war zone. Bodies are everywhere, Boatwrite."

"Yeah, I can see that. Someone had a point to prove and they wasn't playing."

One of the EMTs was yelling out loud from the back of the house, "We got one that's still alive." Detective Boatwrite looked at Detective Flowers when she heard that. That's when the EMTs rushed Big Pete past them on the stretcher, with a mask over his mouth, pumping air into him.

"You got to be fucking kidding me, he's alive still? We need to get to the hospital now, Flowers."

"Come on, let's go." Both of them ran to the car and got inside and drove off, headed to the hospital.

Chapter 36

Porscha was sipping a glass of wine in her backyard. It was dark outside and quiet. She lit her cigar and took a few puffs. That's when her phone started to ring. She looked and saw it was Lil John calling her, she picked up the phone and answered it.

"Hello."

"Good evening, Porscha. How are you this evening?"

"Good, how are you Lil John."

"I'm fine. I was calling to let you know that Big Pete is dead. Lucchese shot him dead personally today, a few hours after the meeting."

"That's good to hear, and I respect the fact you took the time out to call me."

"It takes a lot for an Italian to admit when he is wrong, so this call was a call out for good faith, Porscha."

"And this call means a lot to me and out of good faith, Lil John, I'm not going to tax the families the six thousand dollars, but I am going to keep Manhattan."

"I'll let them know."

"Thank you and you have a blessed night."

"Likewise, Porscha." Porscha hung up the phone as she saw Rakim and Lance walking a man into her backyard with a bag over his head. Porscha stood up and picked her gun up off the table and walked up to them. Rakim kicked the man in his knee, making him drop down to his knees. He then pulled the bag off of his head and Porscha looked dead into Frankie's eyes.

"Where did y'all find him at?"

"Caught him going home," Rakim said.

"You fucking wetback nigga. Lucchese is going to kill you behind this."

"What you thought, you were going to send shooters into my club, kill my workers, shoot at me and all will be forgiven with an apology? Fuck Lucchese. I am the cartel, and it is blood for blood. You must have been stupid or dumb if you thought I was going to let this brush off my shoulders."

"Fuck you. Lucchese is going to kill your ass."

"Not before I kill you. You son of a bitch." Porscha pointed the gun at Frankie's head and pulled the trigger, the sound of the gun blast going off. Blood was spraying out the back of Frankie's head as his body hit the ground.

Porscha looked Lance dead in the eyes. "I don't want nobody to find his body, ever, do I make myself clear?"

"Yeah, you do," Lance said.

"Good." Porscha then turned around and walked off, headed back into her house.

***

"Doctor, it's been three days since our victim was shot. When do you think he will wake up?" Detective Boatwrite asked.

"Detective, he woke up this morning. He's in a private part of the hospital like you asked. He's very weak but he can talk."

"Thank you." Detectives Boatwrite and Flowers walked off to go talk with Big Pete. When they opened the door, Big Pete was lying there with his eyes closed. Detective Flowers hit his foot. Big Pete opened his eyes and looked at them.

"I don't have time to waste, so I'll let your ass know right now. You can play ball, or we can let it be known that your ass is still alive in the ICU at the local hospital. I saw your house and the number they did on it. Someone wants you dead and I don't think they are going to rest until the job is done, so what's it going to be, Pete?" Detective Flowers said.

Big Pete thought about the four families that were going to come at him and Porscha. Most of his guys were dead and the few that were alive were on the run. His only choice was to be a rat. in a low voice Pete said, "I want full protection in Witness Protection, and I will tell you everything you want to know."

"It's good to know you are going to play ball. We will be back, but one question before we leave. Who is Porscha Shields?"

"New York City… she runs all this. She is the head of the Medellin Cartel in New York. I'm not saying nothing else until I get the deal in writing."

"We will be back." They both walked out of the room and looked at each other.

"Flowers, it's time we go talk with Captain Lawson."

"I think you are right, let's go."

***

Trayvon sat in his chair, smoking his cigar and thinking about what Estabon said to him, how killing is a must in the life they live. He also thought about what Judge Adam and Mayor Micheal said, how he is the puppet master and Porscha is the puppet, and he pulls her strings. District Attorney Smith said that he was their little dog before he killed her. He was nobody's little dog or puppet master, the only truth that was told to him was that in the life they live killing is a must. And those were Estabon Sanchez's words. Killing is a must in his lifestyle, but who you kill is your choice. And that's being the boss of the cartel period, and in New York City, he was the fucking boss.

***

"So, let me get this right. Sam Baron, aka Big Pete, agreed to be a CI and rat out all five families in the mafia. Is that what you two are telling me right now?" Captain Lawson asked.

"Not only that, but he also made it clear that Porscha Shields is the head of the Medellin Cartel in New York City. And don't forget we also have Jessica Long, who agreed to be a CI as well against Judge Adam Miller, Mayor Micheal Rapkin, and many others she named.

"Captain, we have two CI's. One ready to go up against the mafia, and the other ready to go up against the government. We have the underworld and Wall Street in the palm of our hands right now. We have the tools to bring them both down, Captain," Detective Boatwrite said.

"We do, but we have to play this right, or we will be on the Missing Person's List."

"So, what do you want us to do, Captain?" Captain Lawson looked into their eyes.

"Wiretaps and video proof on all of them. They want problems, they are now going up against the baddest fucking gang, the NYPD. We going to show them who is really the gorillas in the fucking trenches," Captain Lawson said with a cold grill on his face.

Lock Down Publications and Ca$h Presents
Assisted Publishing Packages

Due to an increase in the price of services we have increased our prices. The prices below reflect the price increase as of 11/01/24.

BASIC PACKAGE	UPGRADED PACKAGE
$699	**$1000**
Editing	Typing
Cover Design	Editing
Formatting	Cover Design
	Formatting
	Upload eBooks to Amazon
	Upload Paperback to Amazon
ADVANCE PACKAGE	**LDP SUPREME PACKAGE**
$1,400	**$1,700**
Typing	Typing
Editing (line editing/content)	Editing (line editing/content)
Cover Design	Cover Design
Formatting	Formatting
Copyright Registration	Copyright Registration
Proofreading	Proofreading
Upload eBooks to Amazon	Set up Amazon Account
Upload Paperback to Amazon	Upload eBooks to Amazon
	Upload Paperback to Amazon
	Advertise on LDP's Amazon and Facebook Page

***Other services available upon request.
Additional charges may apply

Lock Down Publications
P.O. Box 944
Stockbridge, GA 30281-9998
Phone: 470 303-9761
Email: lockdownpublications@gmail.com

Submission Guideline

Submit the first three chapters of your completed manuscript to ldpsubmissions@gmail.com. In the subject line add **Your Book's Title**. The manuscript must be in a Word Doc file and sent as an attachment. Document should be in Times New Roman, double spaced, and in size 12 font. Also, provide your synopsis and full contact information. If sending multiple submissions, they must each be in a separate email.

Have a story but no way to send it electronically? You can still submit to LDP/Ca$h Presents. Send in the first three chapters, written or typed, of your completed manuscript to:

LDP: Submissions Dept
P.O. Box 944
Stockbridge, GA 30281-9998

DO NOT send original manuscript. Must be a duplicate. Provide your synopsis and a cover letter containing your full contact information.

Thanks for considering LDP and Ca$h Presents.

NEW RELEASES

BLOODLINE OF A SAVAGE 1&2
THESE VICIOUS STREETS 1&2
RELENTLESS GOON
RELENTLESS GOON 2
BY PRINCE A. TAUHID

THE BUTTERFLY MAFIA 1-3
BY FUMIYA PAYNE

A THUG'S STREET PRINCESS 1&2
BY MEESHA

CITY OF SMOKE 2
BY MOLOTTI

STEPPERS 1,2&3
THE REAL BADDIES OF CHI-RAQ
BY KING RIO

THE LANE 1&2
BY KEN-KEN SPENCE

THUG OF SPADES 1&2
LOVE IN THE TRENCHES 2
CORNER BOYS
BY COREY ROBINSON

TIL DEATH 3
BY ARYANNA

THE BIRTH OF A GANGSTER 4
BY DELMONT PLAYER

PRODUCT OF THE STREETS 1&2
BY DEMOND "MONEY" ANDERSON

THE DAUGHTER OF A CARTEL BOSS

NO TIME FOR ERROR
BY KEESE

MONEY HUNGRY DEMONS
BY TRANAY ADAMS

Coming Soon from Lock Down Publications/Ca$h Presents

IF YOU CROSS ME ONCE 6
ANGEL V
By Anthony Fields

IMMA DIE BOUT MINE 5
By Aryanna

A THUGS STREET PRINCESS 3
By Meesha

PRODUCT OF THE STREETS 3
By Demond Money Anderson

CORNER BOYS 2
By Corey Robinson

THE MURDER QUEENS 6&7
By Michael Gallon

CITY OF SMOKE 3
By Molotti

CONFESSIONS OF A DOPE BOY
By Nicholas Lock

THA TAKEOVER
By Keith Chandler

BETRAYAL OF A G 2
By Ray Vinci

CRIME BOSS
By Playa Ray

Available Now

RESTRAINING ORDER 1 & 2
By **CA$H & Coffee**

LOVE KNOWS NO BOUNDARIES 1-3
By **Coffee**

RAISED AS A GOON I, II, III & IV
BRED BY THE SLUMS I, II, III
BLAST FOR ME I & II
ROTTEN TO THE CORE I II III
A BRONX TALE I, II, III
DUFFLE BAG CARTEL I II III IV V VI
HEARTLESS GOON I II III IV V
A SAVAGE DOPEBOY I II
DRUG LORDS I II III
CUTTHROAT MAFIA I II
KING OF THE TRENCHES
By **Ghost**

LAY IT DOWN I & II
LAST OF A DYING BREED I II
BLOOD STAINS OF A SHOTTA I & II III
By **Jamaica**

LOYAL TO THE GAME I II III
LIFE OF SIN I, II III
By **TJ & Jelissa**

IF LOVING HIM IS WRONG…I & II
LOVE ME EVEN WHEN IT HURTS I II III
By **Jelissa**

PUSH IT TO THE LIMIT
By **Bre' Hayes**

SAYNOMORE

BLOODY COMMAS I & II
SKI MASK CARTEL I, II & III
KING OF NEW YORK I II, III IV V
RISE TO POWER I II III
COKE KINGS I II III IV V
BORN HEARTLESS I II III IV
KING OF THE TRAP I II
By **T.J. Edwards**

WHEN THE STREETS CLAP BACK I & II III
THE HEART OF A SAVAGE I II III IV
MONEY MAFIA I II
LOYAL TO THE SOIL I II III
By **Jibril Williams**

A DISTINGUISHED THUG STOLE MY HEART I II & III
LOVE SHOULDN'T HURT I II III IV
RENEGADE BOYS 1-4
PAID IN KARMA 1-3
SAVAGE STORMS 1-3
AN UNFORESEEN LOVE 1-3
BABY, I'M WINTERTIME COLD 1-3
A THUG'S STREET PRINCESS 1&2
By **Meesha**

A GANGSTER'S CODE 1-3
A GANGSTER'S SYN 1-3
THE SAVAGE LIFE 1-3
CHAINED TO THE STREETS 1-3
BLOOD ON THE MONEY 1-3
A GANGSTA'S PAIN 1-3
BEAUTIFUL LIES AND UGLY TRUTHS
CHURCH IN THESE STREETS
By **J-Blunt**

CUM FOR ME 1-8
An LDP Erotica Collaboration

174

THE DAUGHTER OF A CARTEL BOSS

BLOOD OF A BOSS 1-5
SHADOWS OF THE GAME
TRAP BASTARD
By **Askari**

THE STREETS BLEED MURDER 1-3
THE HEART OF A GANGSTA 1-3
By **Jerry Jackson**

WHEN A GOOD GIRL GOES BAD
By **Adrienne**

THE COST OF LOYALTY 1-3
By **Kweli**

BRIDE OF A HUSTLA 1-3
THE FETTI GIRLS 1-3
CORRUPTED BY A GANGSTA 1-4
BLINDED BY HIS LOVE
THE PRICE YOU PAY FOR LOVE 1-3
DOPE GIRL MAGIC 1-3
By **Destiny Skai**

A KINGPIN'S AMBITION
A KINGPIN'S AMBITION II
I MURDER FOR THE DOUGH
By **Ambitious**

TRUE SAVAGE 1-7
DOPE BOY MAGIC 1-3
MIDNIGHT CARTEL 1-3
CITY OF KINGZ 1&2
NIGHTMARE ON SILENT AVE
THE PLUG OF LIL MEXICO 1&2
CLASSIC CITY
By **Chris Green**

SAYNOMORE

A GANGSTER'S REVENGE 1-4
THE BOSS MAN'S DAUGHTERS 1-5
A SAVAGE LOVE 1&2
BAE BELONGS TO ME 1&2
A HUSTLER'S DECEIT 1-3
WHAT BAD BITCHES DO 1-3
SOUL OF A MONSTER 1-3
KILL ZONE
A DOPE BOY'S QUEEN 1-3
TIL DEATH 1-3
IMMA DIE BOUT MINE 1-4
By **Aryanna**

A DOPEBOY'S PRAYER
By **Eddie "Wolf" Lee**

THE KING CARTEL 1-3
By **Frank Gresham**

THESE NIGGAS AIN'T LOYAL 1-3
By **Nikki Tee**

GANGSTA SHYT 1-3
By **CATO**

THE ULTIMATE BETRAYAL
By **Phoenix**

BOSS'N UP 1-3
By **Royal Nicole**

I LOVE YOU TO DEATH
By **Destiny J**

I RIDE FOR MY HITTA
I STILL RIDE FOR MY HITTA
By **Misty Holt**

THE DAUGHTER OF A CARTEL BOSS

LOVE & CHASIN' PAPER
By **Qay Crockett**

TO DIE IN VAIN
SINS OF A HUSTLA
By **ASAD**

BROOKLYN HUSTLAZ
By **Boogsy Morina**

BROOKLYN ON LOCK 1 & 2
By **Sonovia**

GANGSTA CITY
By **Teddy Duke**

A DRUG KING AND HIS DIAMOND 1-3
A DOPEMAN'S RICHES
HER MAN, MINE'S TOO 1&2
CASH MONEY HO'S
THE WIFEY I USED TO BE 1&2
PRETTY GIRLS DO NASTY THINGS
By **Nicole Goosby**

LIPSTICK KILLAH 1-3
CRIME OF PASSION 1-3
FRIEND OR FOE 1-3
By **Mimi**

TRAPHOUSE KING 1-3
KINGPIN KILLAZ 1-3
STREET KINGS 1&2
PAID IN BLOOD 1&2
CARTEL KILLAZ 1-3
DOPE GODS 1&2
By **Hood Rich**

THE STREETS ARE CALLING
By **Duquie Wilson**

SAYNOMORE

STEADY MOBBN' 1-3
THE STREETS STAINED MY SOUL 1-3
By **Marcellus Allen**

WHO SHOT YA 1-3
SON OF A DOPE FIEND 1-4
HEAVEN GOT A GHETTO 1&2
SKI MASK MONEY 1&2
By **Renta**

GORILLAZ IN THE BAY 1-4
TEARS OF A GANGSTA 1/&2
3X KRAZY 1&2
STRAIGHT BEAST MODE 1&2
By **DE'KARI**

TRIGGADALE 1-3
MURDA WAS THE CASE 1-3
By **Elijah R. Freeman**

SLAUGHTER GANG 1-3
RUTHLESS HEART 1-3
By **Willie Slaughter**

GOD BLESS THE TRAPPERS 1-3
THESE SCANDALOUS STREETS 1-3
FEAR MY GANGSTA 1-5
THESE STREETS DON'T LOVE NOBODY 1-2
BURY ME A G 1-5
A GANGSTA'S EMPIRE 1-4
THE DOPEMAN'S BODYGAURD 1&2
THE REALEST KILLAZ 1-3
THE LAST OF THE OGS 1-3
By **Tranay Adams**

MARRIED TO A BOSS 1-3
By **Destiny Skai & Chris Green**

THE DAUGHTER OF A CARTEL BOSS

KINGZ OF THE GAME 1-7
CRIME BOSS 1-3
By **Playa Ray**

FUK SHYT
By **Blakk Diamond**

DON'T F#CK WITH MY HEART 1&2
By **Linnea**

ADDICTED TO THE DRAMA 1-3
IN THE ARM OF HIS BOSS
By **Jamila**

LOYALTY AIN'T PROMISED 1&2
By **Keith Williams**

YAYO 1-4
A SHOOTER'S AMBITION 1&2
BRED IN THE GAME
By **S. Allen**

TRAP GOD 1-3
RICH $AVAGE 1-3
MONEY IN THE GRAVE 1-3
CARTEL MONEY
By **Martell Troublesome Bolden**

FOREVER GANGSTA 1&2
GLOCKS ON SATIN SHEETS 1&2
By **Adrian Dulan**

TOE TAGZ 1-4
LEVELS TO THIS SHYT 1&2
IT'S JUST ME AND YOU
By **Ah'Million**

SAYNOMORE

KINGPIN DREAMS 1-3
RAN OFF ON DA PLUG
By **Paper Boi Rari**

THE STREETS MADE ME 1-3
By **Larry D. Wright**

CONFESSIONS OF A GANGSTA 1-4
CONFESSIONS OF A JACKBOY 1-3
CONFESSIONS OF A HITMAN
By **Nicholas Lock**

I'M NOTHING WITHOUT HIS LOVE
SINS OF A THUG
TO THE THUG I LOVED BEFORE
A GANGSTA SAVED XMAS
IN A HUSTLER I TRUST
By **Monet Dragun**

QUIET MONEY 1-3
THUG LIFE 1-3
EXTENDED CLIP 1&2
A GANGSTA'S PARADISE
By **Trai'Quan**

CAUGHT UP IN THE LIFE 1-3
THE STREETS NEVER LET GO 1-3
By **Robert Baptiste**

NEW TO THE GAME 1-3
MONEY, MURDER & MEMORIES 1-3
By **Malik D. Rice**

CREAM 2-3
THE STREETS WILL TALK
By **Yolanda Moore**

THE STREETS WILL NEVER CLOSE 1-3
By **K'ajji**

THE DAUGHTER OF A CARTEL BOSS

LIFE OF A SAVAGE 1-4
A GANGSTA'S QUR'AN 1-4
MURDA SEASON 1-3
GANGLAND CARTEL 1-3
CHI'RAQ GANGSTAS 1-4
KILLERS ON ELM STREET 1-3
JACK BOYZ N DA BRONX 1-3
A DOPEBOY'S DREAM 1-3
JACK BOYS VS DOPE BOYS 1-3
COKE GIRLZ
COKE BOYS
SOSA GANG 1&2
BRONX SAVAGES
BODYMORE KINGPINS
BLOOD OF A GOON
By **Romell Tukes**

CONCRETE KILLA 1-3
VICIOUS LOYALTY 1-3
By **Kingpen**

THE ULTIMATE SACRIFICE 1-6
KHADIFI
IF YOU CROSS ME ONCE 1-3
ANGEL 1-4
IN THE BLINK OF AN EYE
By **Anthony Fields**

THE LIFE OF A HOOD STAR
By **Ca$h & Rashia Wilson**

NIGHTMARES OF A HUSTLA 1-3
BLOOD AND GAMES 1&2
By **King Dream**

GHOST MOB
By **Stilloan Robinson**

SAYNOMORE

HARD AND RUTHLESS 1&2
MOB TOWN 251
THE BILLIONAIRE BENTLEYS 1-3
REAL G'S MOVE IN SILENCE
By **Von Diesel**

MOB TIES 1-7
SOUL OF A HUSTLER, HEART OF A KILLER 1-3
GORILLAZ IN THE TRENCHES
By **SayNoMore**

BODYMORE MURDERLAND 1-3
THE BIRTH OF A GANGSTER 1-4
By **Delmont Player**

FOR THE LOVE OF A BOSS 1&2
By **C. D. Blue**

KILLA KOUNTY 1-5
By **Khufu**

MOBBED UP 1-4
THE BRICK MAN 1-5
THE COCAINE PRINCESS 1-10
STEPPERS 1-3
SUPER GREMLIN 1-4
By **King Rio**

MONEY GAME 1&2
By **Smoove Dolla**

A GANGSTA'S KARMA 1-4
By **FLAME**

KING OF THE TRENCHES 1-3
By **GHOST & TRANAY ADAMS**

THE DAUGHTER OF A CARTEL BOSS

QUEEN OF THE ZOO 1&2
By **Black Migo**

GRIMEY WAYS 1-3
BETRAYAL OF A G
By **Ray Vinci**

XMAS WITH AN ATL SHOOTER
By **Ca$h & Destiny Skai**

KING KILLA 1&2
By **Vincent "Vitto" Holloway**

BETRAYAL OF A THUG 1&2
By **Fre$h**

THE MURDER QUEENS 1-5
By **Michael Gallon**

FOR THE LOVE OF BLOOD 1-4
By **Jamel Mitchell**

HOOD CONSIGLIERE 1&2
NO TIME FOR ERROR
By **Keese**

PROTÉGÉ OF A LEGEND 1&2
LOVE IN THE TRENCHES 1&2
By **Corey Robinson**

THE PLUG'S RUTHLESS DAUGHTER
By **Tony Daniels**

BORN IN THE GRAVE 1-3
CRIME PAYS
By **Self Made Tay**

MOAN IN MY MOUTH
By **XTASY**

SAYNOMORE

TORN BETWEEN A GANGSTER AND A GENTLEMAN
By **J-BLUNT & Miss Kim**

LOYALTY IS EVERYTHING 1-3
CITY OF SMOKE 1&2
By **Molotti**

HERE TODAY GONE TOMORROW 1&2
By **Fly Rock**

WOMEN LIE MEN LIE 1-4
FIFTY SHADES OF SNOW 1-3
STACK BEFORE YOU SPLURGE
GIRLS FALL LIKE DOMINOES
NAÏVE TO THE STREETS
By **ROY MILLIGAN**

PILLOW PRINCESS
By **S. Hawkins**

THE BUTTERFLY MAFIA 1-3
SALUTE MY SAVAGERY 1&2
By **Fumiya Payne**

THE LANE 1&2
By Ken-Ken Spence

THE PUSSY TRAP 1-5
By **Nene Capri**

DIRTY DNA
By **Blaque**

SANCTIFIED AND HORNY
by **XTASY**

BOOKS BY LDP'S CEO, CA$H

TRUST IN NO MAN
TRUST IN NO MAN 2
TRUST IN NO MAN 3
BONDED BY BLOOD
SHORTY GOT A THUG
THUGS CRY
THUGS CRY 2
THUGS CRY 3
TRUST NO BITCH
TRUST NO BITCH 2
TRUST NO BITCH 3
TIL MY CASKET DROPS
RESTRAINING ORDER
RESTRAINING ORDER 2
IN LOVE WITH A CONVICT
LIFE OF A HOOD STAR
XMAS WITH AN ATL SHOOTER

www.ingramcontent.com/pod-product-compliance
Lightning Source LLC
Chambersburg PA
CBHW071213260626
47162CB00004B/1274